C.R.E.A.M.

Lock Down Publications and Ca$h Presents

C.R.E.A.M.

A Novel by *Yolanda Moore*

C.R.E.A.M.

Lock Down Publications
P.O. Box 944
Stockbridge, Ga 30281

Visit our website @
www.lockdownpublications.com

First Edition October 2020
Printed in the United States of America

Lock Down Publications
Like our page on Facebook: Lock Down Publications @
www.facebook.com/lockdownpublications.ldp
Cover design and layout by: **Dynasty Cover Me**
Book interior design by: **Shawn Walker**
Edited by**: Lashonda Johnson**

Stay Connected with Us!

Text **LOCKDOWN** to 22828 to stay up-to-date with new releases, sneak peaks, contests and more…
Thank you.

Submission Guideline.

Submit the first three chapters of your completed manuscript to ldpsubmissions@gmail.com, subject line: Your book's title. The manuscript must be in a .doc file and sent as an attachment. Document should be in Times New Roman, double spaced and in size 12 font. Also, provide your synopsis and full contact information. If sending multiple submissions, they must each be in a separate email.

Have a story but no way to send it electronically? You can still submit to LDP/Ca$h Presents. Send in the first three chapters, written or typed, of your completed manuscript to:

LDP: Submissions Dept
P.O. Box 944
Stockbridge, Ga 30281

DO NOT send original manuscript. Must be a duplicate.

Provide your synopsis and a cover letter containing your full contact information.

Thanks for considering LDP and Ca$h Presents.

PROLOGUE

My name is Cache— pronounced *Cash*— and this is my journey. There are many places I can begin this story. I can start by telling you I'm from Baton Rouge, the capital city of Louisiana, right out the hood. Or shall I say a grimy hood better known as the Southside, AKA, Uptown. Where people are dying daily for something as simple as a pair of shoes. Or where kids never celebrate their father or their mother for that matter. Let's just say so much shit happens where I'm from you wouldn't believe it if you saw it for yourself.

Or I can tell you how I overcame it all and became a hustler's wife. How I'm one day hoping to become a millionaire just to die and not allow my kids to see the struggle like I once had to. Living in a house with twelve other muthafuckas and four of us being my mother's kids. At a very tender age being on my own. Yep, I experienced motherhood young but to be honest that was never my struggle. People, especially adults, always seemed to say having kids will fuck your life up. I used to believe that shit, too, because it had been embedded into my head. No, see, that was a waste of my worries.

To be honest, I'm proud of bringing my kids into the world when I did. Yes, I said *kids*. By the age of 20, I was working on my second child. I must say by that time I was very experienced with what the old folks called *Knocking Boots*. That's not what makes me proud of it all, though. The thing is, if I would not have opened my legs to a man and birthed my children, my mom— whom I found out years later had HIV— would have never had the experience of becoming a grandmother.

Ann was an extraordinary woman, now that I look at it. Don't get me wrong in my book and I'm pretty sure in others as well, she would not be nominated for mother of the year. But the things my mother endured as a woman eventually broke her down. I can only tilt my hat towards her. She might not have been the type of mother on the *Cosby Show* or even the type that tucked us in at night, but what I'm sure of is that she was ours and in her own fucked up way she loved us.

Back in the day, of course, I thought my mother didn't love me, but I was wrong, and going through life proved differently. *Fuck!* After growing up and fighting your way through life, then through incarceration, all that shit goes out the window. *Love* starts to be just what it is, a four-letter word. That is what really makes you endure so much in life. You have to learn to love yourself, especially when you were set up by a muthafucka that used the words, *"I love you"* as freely as everyone else has in your life. Who am I supposed to trust besides me? Not to mention, the fact of being sexually abused in your own home. Being deprived of love so you turn to a nigga in streets with the deepest pockets for security. But watching someone lose their life right in front of your very own eyes and feeling and knowing you didn't pull the trigger, but you went down for it anyway. What kind of justice is that? I believe my time for revenge will come and when it does, all I have to say is niggas and hoes better be careful. I have always been told that it takes a life to save a life, so on this 15-year sentence, I built my momentum. I hate the thought of letting a nigga see me sweat and the only thing on my mind is revenge. That to me is the sweetest thing and I will be damned if I just let a bitch slide and play on my top.

A lot of muthafuckas don't know what I have been through. They just see Cache from the outside looking in and expect everything to be all peaches and cream. Just because I stand a confident 5'7" with bedroom brown eyes. My mocha skin all silky and soft, the kind bitches envied. My ass, of course, fat with thick thighs to accommodate, and good pussy to go along with that, adding the cherry on top. I am the whole fucking package. I also had that kind of sex appeal that Baby Face spoke of. That shit that makes a nigga weak in the knees. As I said that's why bitches see me and think the whole world has been laid at my feet, but if they only knew it's the total opposite. I demanded the world and everything in it to lay down or either get down. The streets taught me that. All this muthafucka had to offer me was heartache and pain. I was once told, *"The pain you feel today is the strength you feel tomorrow."* I'm still waiting for my tomorrow. It's hard to feel and understand where I'm coming from if it's a place you've never been.

C.R.E.A.M.

I hated being broke but I loved when a nigga looked at me as a bitch that money could buy. Just like a thief in the night I never hesitated when it was time to hit them niggas where it hurt, their pockets. That's how I was always able to afford a lavish lifestyle. I didn't come from a family with money. Nope, I didn't come with a silver spoon. I had to fuck my way into riches. I was determined to become privileged. I'm just calling it how it is. I was out there down bad, straight grim reaping shit.

They say all good things come to an end except good pussy. That shit really is hard to come by these days. That said I met a nigga that tied the pussy down. The tables had definitely turned, and I never thought I'd become the victim. I was robbed of something more valuable than money.

Now I know you looking at a bitch all crazy, asking yourself what can be more valuable to a bitch named Cache? My heart is the answer to that question, ladies. I met a nigga named Knowledge. We all know where there is Knowledge you have power, where there is power, you have Cache. I do believe we would have been the next Bey and Jay, but God saw some other shit in my future. Just when I thought everything for me had turned for the better, it was all snatched away. It didn't take long for me to find out that *"Death is not the greatest loss in life."* The greatest loss is what dies inside of us while we live.

CHAPTER 1

"Sister, could you get us something to eat? I feel like I haven't eaten in days!" my baby sister A'nett said, looking at me with her doe-shaped eyes.

I didn't want to deny what she had asked so I got up and peeked out the crack in the door before walking out. *Momma gonna kill me if she knew I came out of the room when she had company*, I thought. For the last time, I looked back at A'nett and I knew I had to take the chance for her. There was no one else fighting for them. I know I am my siblings only hope. Even though I wanted the best for my mom and wished we could have whatever our hearts desired, we'd have to find our own way. The difference between our happiness and the truth, I looked at our circumstances for what it was, the good, the bad and the ugly.

About a year ago we had our first real Christmas staying with our mom, and from the looks of things, our last. No, we didn't have the big forest green Christmas tree with lights that we would have loved to experience putting together as a family. Nope, our Christmas tree had come in the form of a big, tall bookcase which I'm pretty sure my mother's mother—Momo C.W.— was so nice to buy us from her favorite store, St Vincent de Paul.

Well, on that fateful day, we wanted Christmas early and our mother had left us unsupervised. She had gone on one of her, *"I will be right back,"* missions which turned into days. Once again, I was faced to deal with kids who I had started to think of and treat as if they were my own. The reality was I was only a child myself, but I knew there was absolutely nothing I would not do to see the three of my siblings rejoice. I guess that came with being the oldest which made me the captain of the ship.

Being that Christmas I assumed was right around the corner, I decided it would be okay if we opened our presents from *"Paul,"* as my sister Chanel called it. I knew it would distract them for the moment. Two days had passed with my mother out of sight and no food in the fridge so what else could I do to make them happy? The top of the bookless bookshelf seemed so far away, but with the heart of a lion, I knew that if I could make it to the top, all would be okay.

Without further contemplation, I decided to start my race. Barefooted and all I remember crawling up the armrest of the couch, onto the third shelf, fourth, and finally the top. All I remember was being scared but with one swift motion, I knocked at least half of what belonged to us down. As the toys went tumbling so did I. Falling onto my side, I'd been viciously attacked by a rusted nail that had not been hammered into the old Oakwood. I immediately started bleeding.

My sister Chanel was the first to notice that I was *"bleeding to death,"* how she described it, but I knew it would be okay. At that moment I had accomplished what my two sisters and brother needed me to. All I cared about was trying to fill the void so that they would not realize there was one from the jump.

Coming out of my thoughts, I didn't realize that my heart could beat as fast as it was then. I knew my momma would kill me if she caught me out there. Not because she wanted to keep us hidden from the world, but in the hood, to a few our home was considered the jump-off. Where undercover junkies could be junkies and felt safe to come and do their dope, which is how my mom was making a living. So, to see kids running around the house, jumping and making noise would surely not only blow her high but her company's as well.

I quickly grabbed an old jug we used occasionally to transport water to and from. Once that was filled, I grabbed the only thing we had in the fridge which was some sandwich meat. I smiled because this was definitely one of our lucky days. Momo C.W. had not been by in like a week to check on us so that we would be restocked. She always came bearing gifts—food. Even though we had never seen a hot-cooked meal produced in this house yet, she always came through. If only these walls could talk. To be honest, I can never tell how one day Momo C.W. will come with so much stuff and within a day or two everything will be back looking the same, empty. Of course, me, my sisters A'nett and Chanel, along with my brother Carnell talked amongst ourselves and came up with the idea that our mom had to be selling the food. We vowed not to tell a soul because we were too scared that we would get taken away. We loved each other too much for that to happen so we just kept our mouths closed like it was a code of the streets.

Once I safely made it back inside the room without getting caught, I gathered all of us up. We each took a seat on our bed that bared no sheets, eating sandwich meat and taking turns drinking from the same jug without a care in the world. I couldn't help but hurt. The things going on was sad, we were inches away from being homeless under the bridge. Instead of finishing off my sandwich meat, I issued what I had left to them equally. It didn't take long they quickly stuffed the meat in their mouths like I would change my mind. Or like it was the last and in their mind it was. At least for all we knew.

"What can we do now, Cache?" my brother asked.

I really wasn't sure at that moment until I looked up. We all have seen better days, but it's been a while since we've seen a brush, comb, or hair grease. "I have an idea," I said smiling big.

"What you doing, Cache?" my sister Chanel asked, always the one to observe and ask questions.

"I'm 'bout to cut brother's hair but I have something y'all can do," I said, pulling out brown paper bags from the local corner store, and the only three crayons around the house.

We usually would be held up like hostages in our room, coloring on brown bags, and afterward, we would wet them with water from our jug to paste them on the wall. Besides that Christmas, I don't remember too many other things we had to entertain us. Our mom was too busy behind the closed door and we were too hungry to really care what she was doing. The question was does everybody else feel the same?

"Cache, when you cut my hair, I want a Boosie fade with a Steve Harvey line," my little brother said, but his little mind was too small to realize that day it would definitely not happen.

I did the best I could, though. I was so proud of it, too, I called in A'nett next. Once I got to Chanel, it was a different story. She refused to let me cut her hair.

“Come on, I'm a professional. I got this,” I said, trying to convince her.

“No, you don't because A’nett and Carnell look like hairless dogs,” she said, folding her arms and refusing to budge.

“Alright, suit yourself. If you don't want me to do your hair, then I won’t,” I said with my feelings hurt.

Not for long though because my mom stepped into our room with a family meal from Churches. The aroma had me wanting to attack her. I didn't though because I never in my life was I happier than now to see her, or was it because she came with food? Today for her must have been a good day. It had to be because it was not often that she would remember she had four kids to feed. If you asked me, she looked as if she could use the food more than us. She looked sickly. She wasn’t the same woman I remembered so many years ago. I didn’t share my thoughts, though, I just kept them to myself. Same as I do with every emotion I feel. I didn’t know what was going on with my mother. Why she chose the streets over us?

“What in the hell have y'all done in here?” she asked. “Cache, I thought I told you to be in charge.”

“Momma, I put those pretty coloring pictures up,” A’nett said before I had the chance to respond.

“We did it together,” Chanel said, getting mad, trying to compete for attention.

My eyes never left the box of food because I was not sure if it was here to stay.

“Come on y’all, it's time to eat,” my mother said, shaking her head. Her words were like music to my ears. Thank God my sisters distracted her.

Yeah, today had to have been one of her good days because we were allowed out of the room for the whole day. Besides her good days, there are only two of the times we got to come out. When she did not have company or when she was coming right back which turned into a day or two.

Our apartment on Conviction Street was supposedly a two-bedroom. I could not put my right hand on the Bible and testify to that because we were never allowed inside her room. I remember one time we were so hungry I had had enough. Of course, all it took was my sisters and brother to speak those magic words and I would do anything they would ask.

One morning I felt courageous and I decided to go to the unforbidden. Before I could knock on the door, my mom's *friend* Slim came out with sleep still in his eyes.

"What you want, girl? Ya' momma sleep," he said.

I didn't even know he knew my mom had kids. I stood there just looking because I could not find the right words to say. Maybe I was hurt because this man got to spend more time with our mom. I realized for the first time I hated men.

"Girl, speak," he said again, grabbing my attention while I was trying to look behind him. I just wanted to see if my mom was okay and why he came to the door instead.

"We are hungry," I said, slightly ashamed with my head hung low.

"Give me a minute." He walked off and I quickly went back into the room before she caught me.

That day Slim made us pancakes. Our mom never comes out of the room, so I assumed it was okay. I will never forget those pancakes. Neither will Chanel Carnell, or A'nett. Slim's pancakes will forever be embedded in our hearts. I just had to not sleep on Slim. I would hate for dude to think he was going to be father of the year.

CHAPTER 2

It had been a while since we'd seen our mother. Once again it seemed like days. She left us in the house without food, and the only thing we had to eat was half of a watermelon. Of course, that did not last long for four kids. We had eaten the watermelon all the way to the rim and then didn't want anymore because it had soon turned bitter. Earlier that day some kids came by, which also stayed in the apartment complex. Once I realized what I had done and could get in trouble, I had to find a solution to get them out, fast. I started searching the house high and low for things I could give them but what I found left me puzzled. A baby food jar with a glass pipe sticking out of the top. I didn't need my sisters and brother seeing that shit, so I quickly hid it in the top kitchen cabinet out of their reach.

"What's that?" Jerome asked. One of the kids I let in from our complex. He scared the shit out of me.

Mind your damn business," I said trying to stuff the crack jar back into the cabinet, instead, I dropped it. The glass shattered on the floor shattering my heart along with it. I knew I would be getting my ass beat whenever my mom finally came home.

"It looked like a crack pipe if you ask me." He laughed in my face, taunting me. I didn't see shit funny, but he continued, "Yeah, ya mom be round here doing her thang. I overheard my big bro say she the best."

Without thinking and running on pure emotion I grabbed a knife coming straight for his throat. "Don't ever fucking disrespect my mom like that, you pussy bitch!" I screamed, jumping in his face.

Even though I was mad I was also scared, not of him, but of the reality that slapped me in my face about my mom. Never in my life had I felt this much anger and I couldn't trust what I would do if I reacted. Even at this young age, I understood life is 10% what happens to me and the other 90% is how I react to it. As I pressed the knife to his neck my hands trembled.

"Cache, what's going on?" My brother ran in breaking me out my crazed thoughts to see why I was upset.

"Get the fuck out. Now!" I screamed again not bothering to answer my brother. Everything Jerome said about my mother I knew was true. I guess I had been in denial for so long that I didn't want to believe it. Now that the truth was slapped in my face, I knew the real reason I was angry and that was because of the baby food jar and pipe sticking out of it. The truth, no matter how I looked at it and the only person that could change that was my mother. Either that or I needed to accept her shit for what it was, a cloud chaser. Deep down I knew she loved that high so with that thought, I just wondered how much more disappointment I could take from this woman.

I got everything back in order and could finally breathe easily. "Y'all help me push this sofa in front of the door."

It took all of us to do it, but we made it. Even though there was not an adult in sight, with the sofa in front of the door we felt safe. Tired from boredom, we all fell asleep on the sofa.

A few hours later, I woke up to a thin silhouette standing over me. At just a glance I could have thought it was my own shadow. I strained my eyes, trying to see if I could make out who the person could be. So many people came in and out of here, it was kinda hard for me to keep up with them all.

"Slim?" I whispered, hoping my mom was behind him. No, that's not Slim my mind screamed because my words were trapped in my throat. Before I could think of anyone else a hand strongly wrapped around my mouth preventing me from screaming. I could taste blood and knew my lip had been busted. While I was being dragged from the living room into the kitchen, I could hardly breathe I was so scared.

Without making a sound I started crying uncontrollably. He wasted no time ripping my clothes off, exposing my body for him to lust on.

"Please. Please don't do this," I pleaded with him. "God, help me," I said aloud, but not loud enough to wake my sisters and brother. *Where was Ann when I truly needed her?*

"Shut the fuck up because if you wake them other bitches up, including your punk ass little brother. I'ma fuck every one of y'all."

I did what I was told, he didn't have to say no more. I have always and will always protect them at whatever cost. I knew what I had to do, I wouldn't object with his demand, that day I would be the sacrifice. What else could I have done? I just laid there praying to God, any God that would answer my cry. Or at least let this man hurry and get this over with, that would even satisfy me.

As he enjoyed himself moaning in my ear, sweat dripped from his body onto mine. I just kept my eyes straight ahead making sure I didn't make a sound like he told me.

When he was finally done tormenting me and taking what didn't belong to him, he grabbed a dish towel to clean himself. I, however, was still stuck and refused to move. Maybe I thought if I did, he'd come back for more. I also prayed he would keep his promise and not think about touching my sisters and brother.

"You can thank that bitch of a mother that birth you. I would have hurt her instead, but the bitch sick." He laughed like he found something funny because she smoked crack. "Tell that hoe to come with my fucking money or next time I won't be this nice," he said, going into his pockets, throwing some money at me as if that was an act of kindness that justified what he'd done. That's when I noticed for the first time, he wore a black patch over his left eyes. I also knew I would never forget his face. He'd also taught me a valuable lesson. Money wasn't the root of all evil, but men and pussy was. I might not get back at him now or tomorrow, but he was def in my future.

***

When my siblings emerged, our mom still had not returned. I was still stuck in the same spot I had been raped, robbed and taken advantage of.

"Sister, why are you sitting in the dark?" Chanel asked, feeling and looking just as confused as I was.

I quickly pulled myself together, not wanting them to see me that way.

"I'm okay, just waiting on Ann to come back." I tried smiling. I don't know what made me say that, but I regretted it as soon as it came out.

"Well, I'm hungry and if we keep waiting on Ann we'll be waiting forever."

What could I say to that? She was right, even her young mind had accepted we were lonely, and we were all we had. So, why was I the only one waiting around for my mother? I knew they were hungry we had no food. I looked down at the money. *'Patch Eye'* had dropped on me. I instantly had an idea.

After counting the money, I smiled because once again I knew that I would be able to come through.

"What y'all want to eat?" I asked once I was dressed and they were too.

"Pizza," said Chanel.

"Chicken," shouted Carnell.

"I just want to eat, Sissy," A'nett said.

"Alright, let's go," I said peeking out the blinds into the darkness to make sure the coast was clear.

"What are y'all sweet potatoes doing out here? Where is Ann? I know she didn't leave y'all again!" Ms. Monique asked when she opened the door.

I can't really say the her and Ann are friends, but everyone in the complex thought they knew our story. Some people around here are are well off, others are still waiting to see better days. I guess it depends on the person's point of view, and whether they see the glass being half empty or half full.

I could tell by the look on Ms. Monique's face that she thought our whole situation was pitiful. Out of everyone around there, she looked to be the only one that had her shit together. She had a good job, a nice car, and she did not have a whole football team of kids with no daddy present. Every time we came knocking she took us in. Yet, her facial expression told the truth. She looked angry. She seemed to know what went on behind door number 400.

Before Chanel could say anything crazy, I stepped in.

"No. She said she would be back, but we would like to watch a movie and eat," I said like it was okay to just ask other people outside of our house for something to eat. Since she never turned us down, I knew if push came to shove, we had someone we could depend on.

"Come on in," she said, mumbling under her breath about my mom being a deadbeat. If I wasn't on a mission, I would have put her in her place where she belonged.

Once we ate, we watched cartoons and fell asleep once again, but my mind was back on my mission. I silently removed myself from wrapped between my brother and sisters. We slept like this each night and I prayed that they didn't miss my warmth. I slid my feet into my shoes and eased out the door without detection. It had to be like two in the morning, I could tell from the way the moonset. I knew this because of the plenty of restless nights I endured. I watched out of the shattered window for my mom, praying she would come home or wondering if she was safe and tonight was no different. Only this time there was no shattered window, only me and the darkness.

I cautiously walked through the night where only lost souls roamed. Just the sight that surrounded me made me cringe. I couldn't help but wonder if my mom and I would come into contact and if we did, what would I do? Would I overreact like I did when Jerome came at me sideways? I didn't know, I guess if it happened only God Knew what I'd do.

"Ayo, I got that work, lil' mamma?" I heard someone say from an abandoned house.

I just looked but kept it moving. I guess everyone assumed you were a dope fiend when you were out in the streets at this time of night. Before I could get too far, though, I could hear footsteps behind me rapidly approaching. Even though my heart rate was at a thousand, I kept my feet at a steady pace. I was always taught that if you showed any fear the dogs will attack. I kept it cool.

"Damn, lil' momma. You on a mission or something?" As if I didn't hear or see him, I continued to keep to myself.

"Okay, I see how you gon' act. I'm not even tripping, though, I'ma just walk with you." He continued to follow me until our roles were reversed.

At this time, I really didn't know what I wanted to do. Before I left our apartment complex, I thought I had my plan together. Now I was lost and didn't know exactly what it was I'd come for. What I did do was watch every move my *New Friend* made. From where he kept his drugs, who he served and didn't serve. I can't say why I was so drawn to the way he hustled. Maybe it all fell back on my mother and her drug use. All I knew was I wanted to learn everything I could about the game. I knew the type of shit that was happening in the real world, my world, school couldn't give me the knowledge I needed.

"Cache," I finally said when we made it back to where he'd first seen me.

"Damn, lil' momma, that's the first thing you say to a nigga?" he asked.

"That's my name," I simply replied.

"A'ight, I guess I can work with that. Call me Money, then." He smiled.

"No really. C.A.C.H.E. is really my mother's giving." I laughed at him, feeling a little comfortable. I figured if he hadn't done me any harm by now, he wouldn't.

"Damn, that shit's dope, lil' momma. So, what you doing out here, anyway? I mean you too beautiful to be out here at this time of night. Do you know what's all out here? You better be lucky I found you before a copycat Derrick Lee did."

"Boy, whatever." I laughed, slapping his arm.

"Nah, I'm serious these streets are only made for the wicked. If you don't know what's up out here, they'll chew you up and spit you out."

"Maybe you can be my protector." I smiled again at him. I didn't know how to stop, for the first time I looked at a man and knew all men wasn't what I had made them out to be. He seemed sweet and caring and I knew I wanted to see him again. Maybe even for a lifetime.

"Let me start by being your protector and walk you home."

The morning came so fast, but when it did, we were surrounded by so many white people. I didn't know there was so many in this world.

They started asking lots of questions, like, *"Where is your mom? Who can we call to come get you? When is the last time you seen her?"* My young mind could not answer any question. Not that I wanted to either, and in my gut, it was as if my mom was a fugitive off *America's Most Wanted*, I knew something was wrong. I was in shock because I overheard the other white man telling our movie friend if we didn't have anybody to come get us, they would be forced to lock us in a home. Some people might think that being in a *home* might be best for us, especially with children that rarely saw either of their parents, who begged for food, and whose hair was never combed, but from our point of view, we were doing just fine. We might not have had the best, but we had each other. It didn't matter if our mom smoked crack or if we saw her with different men. All that mattered was that we were all together.

That day, though, we didn't leave with the white folks, even though we were all loaded up and ready for takeoff. Momo C.W. pulled up just in time in her shining, all-white cocaine Caddy playing the *Williams Brother's Cooling Water*. At that time, we didn't realize what was going on, all we knew was that we would not get split up. We knew we could look forward to a hot meal, a fresh, hot bath, and a TV with all the cartoons we wanted.

CHAPTER 3

Things suddenly changed for us. For one, getting our hair combed and a haircut for my brother. We were enrolled in school and most of our day consisted of wearing shoes. It was no longer just the four of us. Momo C.W. had kids of her own. Baby Angel was stillborn, and two of my uncles got killed in the war of the streets. One was in Texas, my aunt was in New Orleans, and my mom, only God knew where. Me-Me had her own place and Bri'a did too. Still at home was Bra'lon, Faith, La'mon, and Dia. They were all older than us, so we tried to stay away. We weren't allowed to go into their rooms. Maybe they thought we would steal from them. The only time we were allowed was when they needed us to scratch their heads, backs or playing with their disgusting feet. This shit was so overrated, and I could not take this shit any longer.

Sometimes I thought MoMo C.W. was tired of us, too. We slept in her living room with the couch, chair, and loveseat becoming our beds, but still, we didn't complain. Why would we have when she had taken us in? We should be grateful, right? That was until we realized everyone we were surrounded by, including our friends at school, had moms and dads who were attentive. Buying them the latest shoes and clothes. We noticed they had talked about the movie Blue Bayou for the summer, and the skating rink on the weekends. We had no clue what those things were but what we did know was that we wanted to go to those places, too. Over time I started to become jealous and envious of the other kids but was too afraid to express those feelings. After all, we should be grateful, right? Still no complaining.

One afternoon our mom came to visit us. I remembered being so happy because it had been a while. Maybe this would be the day we could leave with her? I hoped she had her shit together.

"Ann, you coming to get us today?" I asked, calling her by her name. We knew no such thing as a mother.

"No, Cache, not today. As soon as I get a job, I'll be able to get us a house," she said while cooking, which I had no clue she could do.

"Where you gonna work?" I asked curiously.

"Maybe McDonald's," she said unsure. "I don't know."

"Alright, we'll be waiting," I said, believing every word, but that day has yet to come. Our mother-daughter bonding was interrupted by my grandfather, who really wasn't my mom's father.

"Get the fuck out my house!" he shouted.

"For what? I'm talking to my kids!" she shouted right back.

I had to admit I was scared, hurt, and angry. I had never heard anyone talk to Ann like that, not even my father, but I realized I didn't like it one bit. What could I do but stand there?

"I said get the fuck out! You would be able to have ya' kids if you stopped smoking that dope!" he shouted again.

Ann didn't move, and the next thing I knew he had slapped her and spat on my momma. I knew for the second time in my life why I hated men. If only looks could kill. For a moment my mom looked at him with venom. I didn't know what to do, and apparently, no one else did either. I was furious but I dared not say a word.

"I love you, Cache. Tell your sisters and brother for me," my momma said, crying, but now doing what she was told. She was hurt too and ashamed and I understood why.

I looked over at MoMo C.W. hoping my tears would convince her to speak up but she just turned her head. *Hadn't she been through enough as it is*, I thought, but to no avail. No one stopped my mother from walking out the door once again. I wasn't far behind her either, I had packed an overnight bag and was out the door before anyone noticed I was leaving, too. To be honest, I didn't know if they even cared to notice. Out of all my grandmother's kids, I could tell Ann was the black sheep. She was the only crackhead my churchgoing, undercover gangsta family ever had. I wonder if they looked at me the same as if I was headed in her footsteps. Once upon a time, my mother had it together, but I was too young to remember any of it. She also never wanted to talk about the past either and I had no choice but to respect it. My mother is just the way she is. Like they say you can take a girl out of the hood, but you can't take the hood out of the girl.

We had been with our grams for several months now, but all the church in the world couldn't keep me from where my heart desired or take away the fact that being rebellious was in my blood.

My mom still kept her apartment, so whenever I pretended to be in school, I knew chillin' at her spot was safe. Besides now that we didn't live there anymore, I knew she spent less time there and more time running the streets. MoMo C.W. for certain made sure Ann had someplace to lay her head as long as it wasn't under her roof. I guess she felt my mom caused too much trouble and didn't want to be bothered with any of it.

Before I headed her way, I decided to go on the block to see Royal. We'd been seeing each other ever since that night we ran into each other. He'd become my safety net. Someone I could depend on when all else failed.

"Hey, lil' momma, what's up with you? I been checking for yo' ass. Where have you been?" He smiled, giving me a hug. I was glad I put on my best jeans. The ones that showed off my shape. "Damn, you smell good."

"Thank you. I been around, though." I smiled back not wanting to avoid his question. One thing about him he could read straight through me.

"A'ight, that must mean yo grams been having yo' ass in the house. You snuck out?"

"Nah, I'm at my mom's. Don't act like you don't know shit about me, nigga," I said playfully to him.

"I know enough to know you're running from something. You hardly ever disobey yo' people, ma?"

"No, it's not like that I just wanted to spend time with my moms and to see your face," I tried changing the subject because I hated when he could see through my bullshit. I also didn't want to talk about what just occurred back at home either.

"If that's what you trying to convince yo' self then I'm all for it," he said as he continued to watch the block. "Just know I'm here whenever you want to talk about it." He walked off to catch a sell that had just pulled up in a hooptie.

As I always have, since the day that I met him, I watched how smooth he was when it came to making money. He didn't have a crew, he stood alone. He said he didn't need anyone because when he was broke, nobody cared. Now that he's coming up in the streets, they still didn't care but pretended to. That is one of the many lessons he taught me. He also told me he'll never give his money to the next nigga because hustlin' for someone else is like getting robbed without a gun.

From the first day, I met him I knew there was something magnetic between us. Something drew me right to him. Maybe it was his ruthlessness that he tried hiding from me, but I knew the eyes never lie. Or maybe it was because his swag was on a thousand and he still could be a gentleman at the end of the day. I also loved the fact that he was intelligent, which made me love his arrogance. I disliked when a muthafucka was full of themselves and dumb as a box of rocks.

Watching him as I daydreamed, I felt security. As if he protected me from all the ugly in the world. Even with all the dysfunctional despair going on in my life I knew I had finally found my savior. He stuck out like a sore thumb. To the streets, he was known as an animal and if you asked me, I was ready to go out in the jungle with him. Ready to be the Jane to his Tarzan. We all had flaws, some not as beautiful as others, so I respected how he was coming.

"You hungry?" Royal asked when he finally made it back to me.

"I guess I am." What I really was hungry for was him. I just didn't have the balls to admit it.

"You guess?" He looked at me like he knew I was bullshitting. "You know you wanna eat. Acting all shy and shit." He laughed pushing my shoulder.

"And you know you want to feed da baby," I said being a little flirtatious and pushing him back.

After ordering pizza, we ate and chilled at his crib for a while watching the *Equalizer 1.* That is all I remember thinking before I closed my eyes, if heaven felt this good, I'd rather be here in his presence. That was until my dreams were interrupted once Royal tapped me on the shoulder waking me from what I wanted to be my reality.

"Are you ready to go home, lil' momma? It's getting late."

"No—not quite yet. I'd rather spend the night with you. Do you mind?" I asked trying not to look sad.

"A'ight. We can do that, anything for you." He gave me that smile I loved so much.

Without thinking I kissed his lips softly, while he stood above me. I pulled back just to see if he sensed what I felt or if I was tripping.

"You sure?" he asked, knowing exactly what I was asking for.

"Yesss," was all I could say.

To be honest that's all I wanted to say. In an instant, my heartbeat had flowed down from my chest and moved along to my now thumping flower. My soul was on fire for him and I didn't know what I would do if he didn't put this raging fire out. For the first time in my life, I wanted to give myself away. It felt good knowing the sexual act that I craved was all me. He didn't take advantage of me, but, yet I wanted him to if that made any sense.

As he kissed me, I came out of my clothing with no hesitation. I was ready to go hard with him because the option of me going home was out the door. Piece by piece my skin had become exposed to the crisp cool air. We both knew there was no turning back. From my neck, he nipped down to my breasts, from my breasts to my stomach and then to my inner thighs. His tongue started to get real acquainted. I could tell they liked each other too because it had only taken a few hard flicks, licks and sucks for me to explode in his mouth. He drank every drop except the cum that dripped from his mouth. I did the honors by pulling him towards me licking it off his lips. He made me want to taste and see why he excitedly made love to my pussy. The taste from his lips was sweet.

When he thrust inside of me, he had taken my breath. Not because he hadn't taken his time, but because he felt so good inside of me. Once we climaxed almost at the same time all my worries for the moment had vanished. What was far more pleasing to me was him holding me in his arms and I didn't mind if I stayed exactly where I was, at least until it was time to go.

CHAPTER 4

The next morning when I woke up, Royal wasn't on the side of me. I didn't panic or think much into it, maybe he went on the block and trusted me to be in his crib. I got out of the bed to wash up, threw one of his t-shirts on and headed to the kitchen. One thing I learned over the years is how to cook. I could almost make anything enjoyable. I decided I wanted to surprise Royal with a cooked meal. I looked inside the cabinets and fridge to see what I was working with but came up empty.

"This nigga can't be serious, only baking soda? What does he do with this shit? He must eat out," I said aloud realizing this was the life of a grinder.

"He could definitely use someone like me around here." As I continued to search around, I ran across a secret compartment. When I opened it, I shouldn't have been surprised, but I was. I started going through it finding a measuring cup, baggies, a scale, a gun, and a counterfeit machine with money to go along with it. I'm not gonna lie everything inside me was telling me to hit this nigga up, but a small, very small part of me told me not to. Instead, I picked up the gun to examine it. For some reason, this shit excited me. I never saw one in real life only on T.V., so I wanted to see what it felt like in person. It made me feel larger than I am and not in the physical sense.

"What the fuck you doing, ma?"

I jumped, aiming the gun in the direction of the voice. "Fuck! You scared me," I said, trying to laugh it off. I placed the gun back where I'd found it. "I was looking for something to cook to surprise you but came up empty. I just got curious."

He just stood there looking at me with a blank facial expression. I tried reading it but couldn't tell if he was mad or not. My eyes roamed down his body and stopped on his hands. For the first time, I noticed he wore black leather gloves covered in blood.

"I wasn't going to take—"

"The next time you point a gun at someone you shoot and don't ever hesitate," he said, cutting me off.

I looked at him like he was crazy, but I was still curious, so I asked, "Why?" I figured he would tell me what the hell he had gotten himself into.

"That's something you don't ever do. Never ask questions because that gives the other person time to think of his next move. And to answer your question, if you don't shoot to kill, nine times out of ten next time it won't be a next time. Feel me?"

I nodded my head because I did feel him, but I asked myself if I was ever caught up in a situation would I have the heart to bust first? That's a question I'll never get the answer to unless I found myself in that situation. Hopefully, I won't.

"I want you to teach me all that you know," I said out of the blue. I knew my struggle was real because I def didn't choose this life, it chose me.

"A'ight, lil' momma. Let me clean myself up. You ever cooked coke?"

"No."

"Take the Pyrex and baking soda out." He started walking off.

"Pyrex?" I asked, clueless.

"Yeah, the measuring cup."

"Oh, okay. *The Pyrex,*" I repeated.

I did what I was told while he cleaned up. Since he didn't say anything about being covered in blood, neither did I. See no evil, hear no evil, speak no evil.

"We good?' he asked when he stepped back into the kitchen once everything was set up. I didn't know if he was speaking on the blood that once covered him or if I was ready to rock and roll. I nodded anyway and agreed to whatever he was referring to. "Just pay attention to everything that I do. I'm not gonna do much talking so make sure that you do. It's really simple." That was the last thing he said before he got down to business. He put one ounce of coke and seven grams of baking soda into the Pyrex. He then added tap water until it covered the contents inside. He stirred in a circular motion. I watched intensely wanting to know what was so exciting about crack. That shit had my mother so far gone.

"I'ma cook this on forty-five seconds or at least until it's melted," he said breaking my concentration.

Before the beeping sounded, he took it out and stirred it some more. Again, he added a pinch of baking soda. I assumed that should help it dry out, I wasn't sure and didn't dare ask. Once again, he mixed it until it looked like goo. It reminded me of a science project.

"Always run cold water over it once it's done and add two ice cubes inside." He held the Pyrex by the rim and shook it in a circular motion until it was locked up. "Roll some paper towels off and place them there." He pointed out where I should place them. He put the crack on top so that it could dry out. "Now that's how you make straight drop," he said, smiling at his work.

I wondered who had taught him how to cook up crack? His father? His friend? Or did he learn on his own? The struggle had a way of teaching you things when you had no other option. Like so many other times when I held my tongue this time was no different. Royal was a man of few words and more action. The who, what, when and where was not important only the now.

***

Later that night he took me on America Street on the block with him. I'd never been here before so I wasn't too sure why we came. I'd been with him while he hustled, but this time just felt different. Maybe because he was doing for me what he has told me plenty of times that he don't do. He was letting me in. I wondered did that make him a hypocrite?

"You know why I brought you out here, Cache?" The seriousness of his tone made me pay close attention.

"Not really, but I know it was for something. I'm not sure what, but I sure you'll tell me."

For a minute he stood without saying a word. "Women always talking 'bout act like a lady but think like a man. How does a man really think?" he asked, but I'm pretty sure that wasn't a question I was supposed to answer. I knew this was a time for me to listen to the game he spit. "Never think like a man, because most niggas are stupid always think like a Cash because money is what gets you ahead in life and I'm not just speaking of you. Being broke gets you nowhere but having money, beauty and being smart will take you far. Niggas, bitches, hoes and even political muthafuckas respect you when you, gee'd up. The rich and famous only shake hands with their kind.

"Men will always underestimate the power a woman really possesses, but I need you to know pussy is power. Don't let those weak niggas run that bullshit game on you because most of them only get money to get pussy. Do you think Faith would have fucked B.I.G. if he wasn't caked up? She ran circles 'round 'em and the nigga didn't even know it. If you ask me that's the real reason the nigga got knocked off."

For the rest of the night, he gave me the game. He touched on everything I needed to know, from selling dope, selling dreams and selling pussy. He didn't miss a beat, he even told me about robbing niggas and whatever my hustle may be to remember, there is no honor amongst thieves. Never underestimate no one.

"Not even you?" I asked.

He gave me that sinister smile and replied, "Not even me."

The night had begun to slow up. It seemed as if he had served everyone for the night and I was ready to go. I refused to tell him that because his only reply would be "Money over everything. Even sleep lil' momma, I'll sleep when I die." Then he'll try to make light of the situation and say, "Cache, don't rule everything around me," which would only make me blush.

I continued to go with the flow even though I was getting sleepy. My eyes started playing tricks on me and I thought I had seen a red dot on the middle of his chest. Maybe some kids were out playing a game like my Uncle Barilon had done countless times to scare people. Just when that thought subsided something happened. Something unexpected that made Royal grip his chest while his mouth fell open in a perfect O.

"Somebody, help! Help me, oh my God!" That's when he collapsed into my arms. Everything happened so fast, I was so horrified. We both fell to the ground. Where the fuck was muthafuckas when you needed them? Once the gunshots stopped the only commotion going on was my screaming and the now screeching tires on the burning pavement.

***

5 Years Later

It was the night of Oct 25th, I woke up from a horrible dream. It was 4:00 a.m, I was sweating and my heart was pounding, with no one to comfort me. I was hurt, confused and lonely. I held too much anger inside and didn't know how to verbally express it. Flashes of him falling into my arms flooded my memory. I could still see the yellow police tape, blocking off the crime scene. The scent of blood invaded my nostrils as if blood still stained my hands. I didn't stick around that night, I was scared and at that moment felt lonely, so I ran. I guess that's why I constantly questioned my sanity because the shit hurt my soul.

Royal hated the police and so did I. Was it because that's what he wanted me to feel for the police? Or was that a feeling that I felt on my own from all the bullshit cops put out in the Black community? What happened to serve and protect? I could bet that Royal's case was tossed to the side because he was *just another black nigga*! The shit was foul.

I eventually found out through the grapevine the reason Royal had been gunned down. It was said that he killed Lester Groth better known as *'Patch Eye'*. The same man that took it upon himself to violate me in order to settle a debt that was owed by my mother. Two people had lost something that had nothing to do with the situation. I couldn't help but feel Royal losing his life had been my fault. I didn't know how to move on.

All I knew was that the flicker of hope I held in my heart died five years ago right along with him. Sometimes I felt I needed to be with my happiness, but how could I express that I wanted to die that day, too? But I knew my family needed me. Well, at least that's what I told myself and it kept me pushing. My mom had become a full-fledged addict. Every time me and my mom crossed paths, we would both be deeper in the streets. I now understood what was going on. She was knee-deep and could not shake that shit, and in a way so was I.

I started doing whatever it took to provide. I refused to become my mother and I despised broke muthafuckas. From selling drugs, stealing cars, I did what I needed to do but my biggest hustle was men. The way shit was going, I needed to grow up, and fast. I refused to feel those hungry days. Even though my struggle made me strive for more, I vowed to never settle. I had started living two different lives and tried my damnedest to hide what I was doing from my family. Especially my sisters and brother. I knew the things I was doing was wrong and didn't need them to become exposed to the habits I picked up. I also wanted better for Ann, she deserved it. The way I saw it, she had never seen happiness except with my father. Before he died, I could still see a light within her. Now, it was just a light switch and it was flickered off.

As I continued to lay in bed thinking of the past, I realized I had let the sun catch me before I was able to close my eyes. Sleep was definitely not coming to me anytime soon. I decided to get off the couch and take a walk, maybe that would help me clear my conscious. I took a quick shower and threw some clothes on. Before I walked out the door I peeped in on my sisters and brother. I smiled down on them, it made me feel good to know we were still together. Even though I was doing my thing in the streets I always found time to pick them up from Momo C.W.'s to spend time with them. They were getting older and I didn't need them following in my footsteps. I tried as best I could to keep a close eye on them. It was more than what my mother had ever done for us. I made a promise to keep them safe as best as I could and so far, I'd kept my word.

Before I walked out the door, I left money and my keys on the coffee table just in case Chanel needed to get something while I was out. I stepped outside my apartment in the Southside projects. The sun hit my skin and it was very rejuvenating making me appreciate the simple things in life. That was until I looked around the shit hole, I called home, but I dared not complain because having my own space has always been suitable enough for me. *Things will get better in due time,* I thought.

Maybe I'll find a nigga willing to upgrade my ass. I didn't have many options because a nine to five was something I wasn't committing to for the rest of my life. I've seen muthafuckas working for years and still was stuck in the same position.

"Hey, lil' momma. You need a ride?" a dude asked, pulling up on the side of me in a silver Benz.

"Nah, I'm good." I kept walking.

"Don't be like that. It's too hot to be out here and I don't need you passing out on me."

"You wish," I said keeping it short.

"I got money if that's what you worried. I'll pay for it," that nigga had the nerve to say.

His ass was really pissing me off. I hate it when men threw their money around for pussy when so many kids were out here, and struggling mothers could not afford to keep the lights on.

"You know what?" I stopped in my tracks and so did his Benz. "Now you speakin' my kind of language," I told him.

I had a surprise for his ass. Maybe I could teach him a lesson. Even though I was burnt with his trick ass for coming at me like I'm a hooker, I smiled to hide my true intentions.

"Alright, what you waiting on?" He leaned over to push the passenger door open for me with no hesitation.

I slid inside, placing my purse on my lap to keep it closed just in case this nigga tried some slick shit.

"What's ya' name, baby girl?" he asked, touching my leg, making my skin crawl.

"Cache," I answered, knowing I had an agenda.

"Damn, you ain't playing, huh? Lil' mama, off the top you lettin' a nigga know what you came to do through the doe."

I rolled my eyes. "Nigga, that's my given name." I rolled my eyes at his ass.

"And you aggressive?" He smiled. "Yeah, I'ma like you."

"For you, this may be pleasure, but for me, it's business."

"Alright. Fuck it!" For the rest of the ride, we listened to *Meek Mill's Dream Chaser*. It was fine by me, but I knew dude wasn't used to women like me being rude. I could tell he had plenty of women falling at his feet and I was there for his every command. My thing is he served a purpose and if I didn't learn anything from Ann, I learned they were all a means to an end.

CHAPTER 5

We pulled up to a nice house in a middle-class neighborhood. I couldn't help but wonder if this was his mother's house or if it was for one of his sales. A nigga like him loved to stunt. I would not be surprised if this was not his car. It's crazy how men thought life should be lived, but in their mind, you only live once, I guess. Quick to pay for pussy but couldn't pay rent or child support? Kills me. Dude didn't even have the decency to ask my age.

Granted I was well past developed and could put the average video vixen to shame. I guess that's why I don't have any female friends unless they came in the form of my sisters. Women were also afraid I would take what belongs to them if there was ever such a thing. If something or someone is mine, it belongs to me. I was seventeen but looked twenty-five. My breasts were perky, my stomach was flat, my ass was juicy, and the gap between my legs was wide. My face resembled that of an angel thanks to Ann.

As soon as he opened the door, a red nose pit barked and came over, happy to see him. He acted the same, but I hated them, so I hid behind him.

"Give me a minute to put him up," he said realizing I was frightened. Shid, if he wanted any act right, now would be the time.

I stayed on the porch until he went to the back. Once they were out of sight I proceeded to step inside. The place was nice, and I had to admit this shit was laid like you would see in them advertisements for Rooms to Go. If under different circumstances I would have loved and enjoyed the pleasure of coming here. Unfortunately, my shades weren't at all rose-tinted. Life was definitely black and white. I looked around, scoping his shit to see if I had any reason to leave a few windows unlocked so that I could come back and commit a home invasion.

"He outback," he announced, stepping back into the room, bringing me out of my thoughts.

"Cool," I responded. I was still a little shook up, not knowing what else to say but at least I was able to relax a little more since the beast was outside. “Where we doing this at?” I asked, cutting straight to the point.

“Straight, no chaser, huh?”

“I’m a big girl. No need to be baby-fied.” I lifted my dress over my head, standing in nothing but bundles and heels. Compliments of my last caper.

“You must not have any kids.” He looked at my well-developed body. I could very well tell he was mesmerized.

“If I did, it’s none of your concern. Now, again, straight with no chaser. Leave my money on the dresser.” Tricking was the name, not the game, and I didn't come for surprises. This wasn't a birthday party. *Nigga bet not be stingy with the loot. Damn,* I thought while smirking, *I am something.* Yeah, it ain’t like the nigga getting the pussy. I was ready to jack his ass.

He walked closer to me and kissed me passionately like we were newlyweds.

I pushed him back. “I need a drink,” I said. Without permission, I headed for the kitchen which I could clearly see.

“Help ya self, let me grab a rubber.”

As soon as he went upstairs, I headed back to my purse to grab the crushed Xanax I always carry. I opened his fridge and luckily found a Coke to go with the Henny. After fixing the drinks I dumped more than enough of the powder-substance using my finger to mix it up. As for me, a glass of Coke would be just fine! I could hear him coming so I had to dump the powder inside one of the million boxes of Captain Crunch cereal boxes. This nigga loved cereal. I gave him his drink and we both downed them. Unknown to him, he would not be feeling this sweet, hot pussy today.

I smiled at him devilishly, grabbing his now empty cup and sitting them in the sink. “Let’s go.” I grabbed him by the hand, letting him lead the way.

Once we entered the room, he wasted no time in coming out of everything but his socks. There was no way I was fucking that dick. That nigga was built like a horse! Then, for that shit to be damn near to his knees. I instantly started praying that the fucking pill kicked in soon. I wasn't even sure if I could put it in my mouth but it if need be—

"Oh, cat got your tongue now, huh?" He smirked like he knew he had a bitch cornered.

"Nigga, put that money on the dresser."

Once that was done, I eyeballed the money and knew his stuntin' ass was a big spender. He started stroking his shit as if he was trying to come on his own which would have been fine by me. Right then and there I knew if this nigga was passed out or not, he was not about to damage me down below. As if I was getting ready to pray, I hit my knees and let my mouth do the talking. To my surprise, my forehead was almost touching the base of his stomach.

"That's right, bitch, swallow that shit," he said, grabbing my hair which pissed me off even more.

I usually could hit a nigga off in under five minutes, but this nigga would stop me as soon as he was about to explode. *That's cool, though. Nigga take your time*, I thought. *Fuck it. I will just have to suck it until he was out for the count.*

I fucked up though when I placed his nuts in my mouth while still stroking. He exploded everywhere. I stuck the tip of my finger in his box.

"What the fuck you doing to me?" he moaned. It definitely wasn't a refusal.

"That's right, daddy, let that shit flow. Make that dick cum for me. Fuck! That shit making my pussy so wet," I said, talking shit, but at the same time, I love when a nigga bowed down to me. As I encouraged him, the nigga kept cumming so much the shit ended up in my hair.

To catch his breath, he laid back on the bed. "Where you going? We ain't finished."

Muthafucka, you should be out, right now. "I'm going to clean myself up," I said, walking in the bathroom without his permission. "I hate greedy niggas."

"You said something, little momma?"

"Nah!" I slammed the door. *"What have I gotten myself into?"* I thought out loud. "This is nothing to you, girl. Do what you have to and get out," I coached.

I took my time because I didn't want to fuck his ass. This nigga should be asleep by now. *Boom! Boom! Boom!* I jumped. *His ass straight tripping.* "I'm coming, damn!" I said, aggravated. "Give me a fuck—"

I was cut off when I swung the door open. I was face-to-face with a gun and someone behind a ski mask. I quickly threw my hands up. I looked toward the bed and his big, dumb ass had finally passed out. I regretted drugging his ass.

"Get the fuck on the bed, bitch!"

I did with no hesitation. From the voice, I knew I was dealing with a woman. Bitches are vindictive. *She might be one of his hoes. Damn, I hope I get out of this shit alive*. I started regretting coming here. I would rather ride the nigga dick than to have a gun pointed at my head any day.

"Where the nigga pants?" I pointed. She grabbed them and came out of each pocket with money wrapped in rubber bands. "Where that nigga keep the safe? I know he got one."

That's when I had an idea. I didn't know if it would work but fuck it. What did I really have to lose? "Let me help you," I said. This bitch started laughing. "What the fuck funny?" I asked.

"You, bitch. I've never seen someone with a gun in their face and still trying to hustle. You got heart, Ma." She pulled off the mask. No homo but this hoe was beautiful. "I'm One of a Kind." She smiled. "But call me One." She tossed me some rope and duct tape.

"I'm Cache," I said. "What you want me to do with this?" I was confused. In movies, I have seen where the robber makes the victim tie themselves up.

"Tie that nigga up. We don't need him to wake up from whatever it is you gave him."

How the fuck she know that?

"Oh, don't worry. I'm not psychic. I was hiding in the kitchen pantry." She smiled.

After his ass was tied up, we started flipping shit, looking everywhere, under the bed, knocking loose floorboards, running up in other rooms and we still came up empty-handed. We didn't find anything. We came up empty but at least we hit his pockets for something.

"Let's bounce," One said.

"Cool but let me grab my shit out the cereal box." I didn't have to tell her what I was talking about since I know she was watching me. "Bitch, check this shit out!" I shouted, wondering how I missed this. I came out of the box with stacks, nothing compared to what he carried on him. I went in the next box, then the next, and they were all turning up with—*Cache* and a gun.

I just hoped that I could trust this bitch. After having a gun in my face, it was kinda hard for me to trust when just a minute ago she was ready to blow my brains over the nigga dick.

"Should I do to her what she'd done to me?" I asked myself looking at the gun I'd found.

The next time you point a gun at someone you shoot and don't ever hesitate. That gives the other person time to think of his next move. Royal's words echoed loud in my head. For a second, I thought about jacking her ass to let her see how the shit felt. I didn't know her, and she didn't know who the fuck I was. Only for a second, my mind went there, I decided to tuck the gun in my purse, for now.

"Oh, One, come through!" I yelled to get her attention.

"What's up, Cache?" she said my name like we were cool like that. "Why you in this bitch all loud and shi—" She stopped midway, once she saw all the money I had emptied out the boxes.

One quickly grabbed a black trash bag and every fucking cereal box insight was thrown in. Once that was done, I grabbed the nigga's keys and we got the fuck out. I knew right then and there I was rolling with One. My mother didn't name me Cache for nothing.

I just prayed Royal's words never came back to bite me in the ass. *The real gone ride, the fake gone divide.* I thought once again about the many lessons that were handed to me.

CHAPTER 6

New Orleans

"Cache, the hottest chick under the sun." I turned to see One prancing towards me in some Gucci heels and a silk robe which I was sure was Gucci, too. Under the robe were a bra and lace thong. Those heels were bad, but I couldn't dare walk in them.

I had been sitting outside by the pool in some heels and a Chanel two-piece, smoking a blunt and enjoying the sunrays. "Hey boo." I smiled.

For the last few months since I been kicking with One, shit for us had been nothing but love. I can't even front or lie money has been falling in my lap like it's raining from the sky. I always saw myself getting ahead of the game by becoming the next hustler's wife, but this shit right here was on a whole other level. If you asked me it was better than being a nigga's trophy. I love the freedom of being able to spend what I wanted when I wanted. The only time I asked a nigga for money was when I demanded him to give up the combination to the safe.

"Girl, you holding out I see. You somethin' shiesty with the Dro. You the only one I know that don't like to puff-puff-pass," she said, extending her manicured hand toward me to take the blunt.

"You the only one I know that don't like to buy and allow a bitch to play puff-puff-pass," I said laughing because that hoe didn't like to spend her money on weed.

"Look, I was thinking about this party tonight. There better be some hot niggas in this bitch."

I changed the subject to a more serious one. "Girl, you know, hands down, the party is the hottest ticket in the city tonight."

"Bitch, it better be. I paid twenty-five hundred dollars for these shits. Each," she said, referring to the tickets.

"Damn, bitch, I'ma pay you back. As much of my weed, you smoke, you need to be paying my ass."

"I'ma pay ya' ass back, alright, with my foot up ya' ass."

"With what? Ya' tongue up my ass?"

She laughed. "You wish, but don't tempt me. For the right amount, you know anything possible."

***

Harris Casino, Canal Street

Later that night, I was dressed in Ferragamo heels with an Etro gown, mimicking what Elsa Hosk donned at the premiere of A Hidden Life. Of course, you know One came with it. She was clad in a Swarovski beaded Atelier Versace gown. These bitches couldn't stand either side of us, the back or front either. I mean, I ain't trying to toot my own horn but we came to slay. Bitches like us didn't get to play dress up like the hoes in Hollywood.

We made our way through the place, watching who placed the highest bid on roulette, blackjack, and craps tables. Shit, we even watched the slot machines. You never know. Can you say Sugar Daddy? I spotted a few potentials with a thousand chips. The house was filled with entrepreneurs, athletes, entertainers, and hustlas included. Anybody could get it.

"May I help you with a drink?" A waiter with a tray filled with bubbly asked. If the nigga had a better choice in careers he would be got.

"Thanks." I grabbed two. One for me and the other for One.

Before taking a sip of the bubbly, I got distracted, catching eyes with this dude off in a dark corner. I checked him out inconspicuously from head to toe. The nigga was laced. Everything about him as far as I could see was official. From his tailormade suit all the way down to his loafers the nigga was together. My pussy had instantly become so wet that the seat of my black lace panties began to moist with my cream.

"One—don't look now but there is a dude at my six."

"Nigga looks paid," she said, looking away.

"What the fuck? Nigga acts like he knows us," I said, hoping he wasn't one of our vics.

“Don't panic, I'm going to fuck with him. What better way to find out what's going on than to ask?” she said, walking off before I could stop her.

That damn girl, I swear, had too much heart, I thought, shaking my head. I took a seat at the bar not knowing what else to do but nurse a drink.

“You too beautiful to be sitting here alone. If you were mine, you would’ve never been here by yourself,” someone whispered in my ear.

I turned around to see a handsome, chocolate face with pearly white teeth and a smile that could make me bend over backward. “Never judge a book by its cover. I could be the next Hugh Heifer with a stable full of dicks. Maybe this is where I choose to be left alone.” I smiled back.

“I’m Thadius.” He extended his hand. “I would ask to join that stable but I’m too selfish to share.”

“Anna.” I gave him my hand along with a false name. He took my hand, placing a kiss on top. “I see you’re a gentleman.”

“I try to be,” he said, giving me that smile again, taking the seat next to me. “So, what’s your story? Your girl told me you was interested. Are you?”

This bitch, I thought with a smile on my face.

“We’re moving a little fast, huh? What time do we have to waste? I would hate for the clock to strike midnight which would leave you running off in the night without your glass shoe.”

“If that’s the case, we skip that part and move on to taking off our clothes. Oh, and for the future, that’s Cinderella shit is so corny. You can’t come up with nothing better than that?”

“You right, but I’m sure you’re used to making men say lots of things that don’t make sense. Especially when you’re speaking of taking clothes off. I love when a woman knows what it is, she wants.”

“You right about the making men say lots of things,” I said. *Nothing wrong with a little flirtation.*

“Now that’s too conceited.” We laughed. “Would you like another drink?”

“Sure, Long Island will be fine.”

He beckoned for the barmaid and ordered my drink.

"No, seriously, I came here with my girl," I said, and he started looking around.

"Oh, it's that type of party? Damn, so that means I don't stand a chance, huh?" He asked just when One walked up.

"A chance for what?" she asked.

"For whatever," he responded.

One looked at me curiously. I slightly nodded, letting her know he was a possibility. "I don't think you can handle whatever," One teased, taking his olive out his drink, surprising me, placing it in her mouth.

We had never done anything close to a threesome. One of us would either lure our vic into the rooms or go home with them, spike their drinks and go from there. I absolutely wanted to know where she was headed with this.

"Let's find out," he challenged. He stood up, placing his hands in his pockets to hide his growing erection. For the most part, we didn't have to fuck the men unless it came down to it. Or if we just simply wanted to. "My place isn't too far from here. I can either arrange a car to pick y'all up or—"

"No, just give us the address. We'll be there shortly," I said.

"Cool. We'll meet up at midnight, Cinderella. Have a nice night," he said, giving me the address.

"Girl, what the fuck? I thought either of us would go in and spike his drink."

"Damn, can a bitch have a lil' fun? You know we don't get much dick as is. Everything is always a job."

"Aight, cool, but you know I don't be with all that gay shit."

"Look, I have some coke so you can relax and calm your nerves."

We walked to the ladies room to *powder* our noses.

"You know we haven't hit the strip club in a while. What's up with that?" I asked while she took the coke and made lines.

"If you want, we can do that tomorrow before we bounce, because it's too much money to be made. You know I'm never turning a dolla down," she said before snorting a line of coke.

I had my bill already rolled to do me next. When I came up, I threw my head back, pinching the bridge of my nose. My eyes started to water from the coke burning my nose as the drainage tickled my throat. I don't think that's a feeling I'll ever grow to love. We put everything up and cleaned our nose before we left the bathroom.

An hour later we were lit and ready to go.

"You ready?" she asked.

It was about that time. Always riding in separate cars on the job, we waited on valet parking to bring our cars around.

Before going to our destination, we went back to our hotel room to change. Thirty minutes later we pulled into a suburban area just outside the city. It was just after midnight so the streets were quiet. We didn't need anyone to place us in the area. This was a nice neighborhood. Unlike in the hood, these uptight bitches were probably peeking out the window with one hand and a phone in the other one, playing neighborhood watch.

"Girl, this shit nice," One said with a glaze in her eyes.

"Fucking right. You know the rules. We out this bitch in an hour, no later than two. So, if you get ya' back blew out or not, we bouncing."

"Ten-four."

We knocked on the door and not even a minute later we were walking inside.

"Welcome, I'm glad y'all made it." He smiled.

He stepped to the side allowing us inside his home. Damn this nigga's shit was tight. *We really hit the jackpot with this one*, I thought. There were plenty of times we ran into some niggas that looked as if they owned a bankroll, but when all the shit was said and done the nigga would end up bringing us to his momma's crib.

I took him in, he was now in silk PJs and shirtless. I had to admit dude was killing me and the only way to revive me was if he fucked me back to life. One dropped her bag and we both dropped our trench coats at the door. We came prepared with much of nothing to take off. Whenever on a job, we transformed, converting into business mode, becoming alert to our surroundings. Never know what kind of trap we could be entering.

"What about a drink?" he asked both of us, walking to his minibar.

"Sure," we both said.

He fixed us all a shot of Patron. I watched closely because I would hate to become prey. He was the type of nigga you couldn't trust. Look at the Green River Killer, on the outside shit looked sweet, but his ass was killing hoes for a hobby.

"Where is the music?" One asked before he tossed her the remote.

I already spotted the safe behind the bar. I instantly started thinking about how we would get him to let us inside.

One placed the music on *Usher's Seduction* and the music blended in right along with the dimmed lights. On our second drink, I started to feel a little tipsy. I knew that was my limit, I needed to stay focus. Becoming sloppy wasn't good for business.

Thadius took a seat on his sectional while both of us stood in front of him. I could tell One was ready, but I wasn't too sure. Being the leader that she was born to be she took the lead. She gently grabbed me by the side of my face and neck, how a man would, and kissed me. I did not pull back either. *It's all for a cause*, I told myself. I grabbed her waist, pulling her toward me and I had to admit her soft body felt nice against mine. She cupped my breasts, rubbing it through my black lace bra, flicking her thumb across my nipple. The Patron and coke mixed had my hormones raging in overdrive.

Out the corner of my eye, I could see Thadius sipping on his drink, stroking his big, chocolate dick. Dude was packing and I couldn't wait to climb on top. One moved down with her hand and mouth, sucking on my neck, and her hand now rubbing over the fabric between my legs.

"Fuck," I moaned, not being able to stop myself.

"Lay down," she demanded, and I did, on top of a soft white rug.

She slid my panties off, tossing them to the side. I removed my bra and she followed suit. She looked at my body, taking it in, and

I got the feeling she was enjoying herself. She rubbed my stomach, moved down to my box, spreading my lips to rub my clit in a circular motion, making my back arch. I looked over at him wondering what was taking him so long to join. He had taken out his phone to record us. At the moment, I let it slide but made a mental note to break that shit.

"I want you to taste her," he said.

Now I don't know what I expected, maybe for One to start tripping or some shit, but she definitely surprised me. She smiled at me, and before I could object, she dove in headfirst.

"Do you mind if I join?" he asked me.

"Come," was all I was able to get out before I started shaking.

Stepping out his pants he got behind One with his phone still in hand. His dick looked so hard. Without warning, he thrust deeply inside her walls. For a moment she stopped making love to my box but not for long. I could tell he was putting that pressure on the P. Deep, long and wide was how he fucked her, and the shit turned me on. I couldn't take it anymore, and for the first time in my life, I squirted all over One's face.

She didn't stop and neither did I. I felt demon-possessed as I continued to cum. My body had turned on me and even though I did exactly what I said I wouldn't do for the moment I was under her spell. What she made my body do was phenomenal.

"You fucking bitch, yesss," I hissed like a snake and rolling my body like one as well.

"You like that?" she asked, smiling while looking up at me.

This hoe knew exactly what she was doing to me and if her head wasn't so good, I'd slap that smirk right off her face. Again, she moved her tongue over my clit just how my body needed her to as if they spoke a language of their own. I was weak in the knees. The only thing on my mind was straight penetration.

One grabbed the bag of X pills. "Turn around," she told me, placing a pill on the tip of her tongue, sliding it in my ass.

Thadius laid back this time and for the life of me, I couldn't understand how this nigga still stood at attention.

"Ride his dick," she told me. "My turn." She smiled.

I wrapped my legs around his waist, sliding on him with ease. "Yes," I moaned, riding him like a cowgirl.

While he had his tongue out, she placed a pill on the tip also, straddling his face, easing on his hard tongue. We both jerked, fucking him, kissing each other until we came together. I was so spent, rolling out my mind. Never in my life had I been fucked the way that I have tonight. I don't know how things would be between me and One after tonight. I just hoped things weren't uncomfortable with us. As we laid there trying to catch our breath, Thadius got up, lit a cigarette, and proceeded behind the minibar to his safe.

We can't be this lucky, I thought, nudging One getting her attention. "Bitch, can you see the number he punchin' in the safe?" I whispered to her.

"Don't worry 'bout a thing. We don't need it," she said, slipping out of her heels before standing up.

I had no clue what this girl was up to, but I followed suit.

She tiptoed over to the duffle bag we came with and came out with something nasty. A gun. I quickly got up because I knew shit was about to pop off. Good sex or not, money was the game we played and played it well.

"I really enjoyed myself tonight. We should do this more often," he said turning around, but he never made eye contact.

Boom! One shot him in the head without thinking twice.

"What the fuck?" I asked in shock. If I was high, I wasn't anymore.

"No reason to cry over spilled milk. Let's get this bag and bounce."

"Bitch, you didn't have to kill him. Fuck!" I said panicking.

"That nigga shouldn't have good dick. No way was I letting this nigga slang dick like that," this bitch had the nerve to say. I knew she was losing her fucking mind. She grabbed the duffle and emptied its contents which was old newspapers. She went to the safe and started pushing everything inside the bag.

I stood there in shock, my mind on a thousand and I couldn't think straight. I thought back to that night five years ago when Royal was killed. It was like no matter how hard I tried I couldn't escape murder and mayhem. I knew someone would want justice. He had to have a family, right? By any means, I didn't want this shit coming back on me.

"What I need to do?" I asked realizing the consequences and repercussions of our actions that could surely find their way back to us.

"Don't forget to grab that nigga's phone and the two glasses we drunk out of. Anything you think our DNA is on, snatch it up or wipe it down." I did exactly what I was told. No reason for me to just stand there. As silly as it may seem I even wiped the nigga's dick off. That's how careless I was fucking the nigga without a rubber.

"Let's go," she said, and just like that, we had committed murder.

CHAPTER 7

"Damn, bitch. So, you been ducked off out here? Had me looking for your ass high and low with a flashlight."

Now I know One is only herself but something inside of me made me feel she had a hidden message between those words. I didn't need this bitch to wild out on me. I was still spooked, but I wouldn't dare tell her no shit like that, so I pulled myself together.

"Now, you know it ain't even like that between the two of us. Why you always got to be extra? I only came to get a piece of mind."

"*A piece of mind*? From what?" she asked scrunching her face like I said something out of pocket. As if she'd erased what happened last night.

"Yeah. What's wrong with that? You ever thought about getting out of this life, seeing more than these grimy streets? I'm tired of hustlin'. I used to love this shit, though. Sometimes I wish I had a million dolla nigga. I be straight praying for a miracle. Where offset when ya' need him?" I didn't want to tell her I was buggin' from the shit she pulled off last night. I mean, where I'm from, the shit happens every day, but to be caught up in this shit is a different story.

"Girl, please. This is my life and I ain't got time to pray. Especially when God isn't the one makin' it rain," she said, hitting the blunt like she owned it. "Now, if you'll excuse me, I have a few lap dances to tend to. My miracle is right inside there, and fuck Offset. I'm tryna get at the nigga Onset." She never missed an opportunity to hit a nigga's pockets.

This dancing shit was still new to me. I mean, it all paid the bills, so really, I couldn't complain. Plus, we didn't do this too much. When she left me alone, I was subjected to fall right back into my sabotaging thoughts. I cannot deny that the money I made was well worth the hours I put in. What I am tired of is the lifestyle. Now murder could be added to my jacket, even though I didn't pull the trigger myself. I might as well had because I didn't do anything to stop it. I have always thought about my future, but with the lack of education I possessed, the only place I could find employment was the streets, hittin' these niggas. I must admit I was doing well. Even though I wanted more out of life, I couldn't complain. I just looked at it as if God blessed me with this body. Why not use it to pay the bills?

"Cache, girl, Kane is in here having a fit! You go on in ten, so get ready before he starts docking our pay!" Juicy yelled in the door, slamming it before I got a chance to respond.

I continued to smoke my Dro, disregarding everything Juicy said. I might not have an education, but money is something I could count even if I was blind. Having that thought, I'm convinced the money flow is because of me. The men and women flooded the club all because of Cache. I shut shit down whenever I came to the city, and I needed Kane to remember that. After finishing my blunt, I tossed it and stomped it out with my Red Bottoms. Everyone knew when I was in town. I demand attention and needed every one of my tricks to feel special and to know if I'm needed, I'm there.

As they played *Lil Wayne and Kelly Rowland's Motivation*, I worked my hips professionally up and down the pole like a duck takes to water. I knew what they wanted so I gave it to them. They started throwing money as if their pockets ran longer than the Mississippi River, and I loved every bit of it. Even though the pole paid me well, the real money for me was on the floor. I looked around, casing the place for my next victim. I spotted One of a Kind in the back, tootin' Coke and it made my stomach cringe. Not because I'm against it, but I needed a hit like yesterday!

I started fucking with Coke not long after meeting One. The same shit I swore to never do. My first hit was amazing and no matter how much I put into my body, I could never get that first high. It all started when she introduced me to the stage. One told me that I would be relaxed, and I would have the strength and confidence of Superman. This shit was new to me showing my body in front of hungry men. I had a little stage fright and she told me the coke would do just the trick to erase my fears.

She was only a year older than me. She had already become a product of her environment. The streets weren't that kind to her and even though she is still a beautiful girl you could see in her eyes that life had not been that easy. That only made her live life care-free with no regrets. As for me, I have seen the streets break my mom down piece by piece, but it didn't make a difference. They say a hard head makes a soft ass and I guess I'll have to fall to see if any of it's true. I still wanted a hit. I had it all under control.

No way would I ever let shit fall apart like her. I only used *when working*. They say make money and don't let it make you. I have my shit together and I refuse to let my drug-use dominate me. After finishing up my set I grabbed my money from the stage and stuffed my earnings into my Purple Crown Royal bag. I hurried off the stage, headed to the locker room to put my cash up. No need to carry it around. I love filling empty bags!

"Girl, you heard about my lil' potnah getting knocked?"

"Girl, who?" was what I heard when I entered the locker room.

Peaches and Cream always knew somebody who knew somebody who always ended up being their *"lil potnah"*. I wouldn't be surprised if Peaches didn't know the person at all. Them two hoes was always in somebody's business, and if they didn't have anything on you, they would make some shit up that sounded good. Sometimes I think them hoes love to hear themselves talk.

"You know Fendi? She be in them stores stealing. When I tell you, she been snatching everything that's not nailed down." They both high-fived and laughed like there was something to celebrated.

I just shook my head and kept going. *Straight bums*. As I'm inside my locker I feel someone walk up to me, pressing their body to mine. *I hope it's not One*. "What the—" I turned around, ready to go to war. "Of course, it is your pussy sucking ass."

"Chill, mami," Angel, this Spanish chick said. "Why you always gotta be rowdy? Act like a lady sometimes."

"Girl, bye." I held my hand up, pushing her out my way.

"So, you still acting bad, huh? You'll give in just like ya' girl One did. Y'all always do. Just watch and see. Ask ya' girl how that pressure feel. What Angel wants, Angel gets, homes."

I headed out the dressing room refusing to entertain her foolishness. Gay or not, her money didn't compare so she had no chance in hell. I headed up to the VIP section where I knew One would be. I wanted to get high and I knew she had what I needed.

"Dang bitch, what took you so long?" One questioned me when I approached her section. "You know the real cash flow don't come until Cache comes."

"That's what she said."

We laughed at our inside joke, not caring if no one else but us got it. I took a seat on the other side of this dude named Zane while she passed me the coke. I decided not to mention Angel afraid that One would flip, and I didn't need any of that shit.

"Why you can't let this devil go, ma? You too pretty for this shit," Zane said.

"The same reason you always trying to spit that, *My Brother's Keeper* shit, but you out here selling this same stuff, being a hypocrite. Let me do me for now and holla at me later when you get a nine to five instead of putting this same devil you are speaking of into our black communities," I told him right before snorting a line. I threw my head back and waited for that euphoric feeling that was certainly to come.

"Zane, don't come over here with them Malcolm X speeches. Why niggas always got to blow it? Dang! We all know all you muthafuckas want is the goodies, but it just seems lame when you try to play Captain Save A Hoe. You the one sold me the shit, now you stuntin' for my girl? Relax, you might get it for free," One said.

"I doubt that," I said falling into my own zone. Every time I got on that coke, I felt invisible, and this time was no different. Nothing in this world to me mattered. "What's up, y'all? Where the real party at? I get off in five minutes." I looked back and forth between the two dudes, then my girl.

"That's what we was just spittin' to One. We tryna see if y'all trying to make some extra money?" this stud name Ryleigh asked.

"Bitch, please, you know it ain't trickin' if you got it. Do you? 'Cause the last I heard, them Brookstown boys were bird-feeding you."

Everyone laughed that had ears in the VIP section. I get a lil' feisty and loose-lipped when I'm on that coke, straight feeling myself.

“Fuck it. She might not be able to put her money where her mouth is, but I can. So, what's up?” Zane asked, pulling out a knot I couldn't refuse. Everyone else looked at Zane like he was crazy. The nigga never offered to pay for pussy.

“See, now that's what I'm talkin’ about. Now you speaking my kind of language. For the right price, I'll put this pussy where ya’ mouth is.” On some real shit, I really felt hurt because he’d just proven to me that he is no different from every other disrespectful motherfucker in my life. I just grabbed my drink, downed it and prepared to go. Like I said, this life paid the bills.

CHAPTER 8

"Girl, I know one thing, these niggas better be poppin' it off because I could be doing something better with my life," I told One. I wanted to back out now because her ass had me traumatized.

"Better like what? You know darn well we gettin' that bag, even if we gotta take it. By all means, I gotta get mine, ya' heard!" She laughed, but I knew she was always true to her word.

I just didn't need a repeat, murder was definitely not my thing. But we took care of each other, we all we had. I knew it wasn't by chance that God put us together. We both came from the same kind of horrific backgrounds. Sometimes I think she loved this life more than anything else in this world, including the money. Me? I wanted more! I just hadn't figured out what more was. I definitely could see myself doing better but actions spoke louder than words. As of now, I knew one thing for sure—I'ma milk the game for all it was worth.

"So, how much you got tonight?" I asked trying to change the subject.

"On which job?" she asked, referring to the club or our side job hittin' pockets.

"Both," I answered, really wanting to know.

"Girl, the dance floor was poppin', so I hit a lick. I got thirty-five hundred from that, and from the stage, I got to stack. As for the pockets, I hit for a Black Card. That shit didn't come cheap, though. I gave the fat, greasy ass nigga a handjob. But fuck it, I got the nigga's card and a bill-fifty."

"Girl, sound like we going on a shopping spree. Don't forget we gotta pop Tara and Regan off." The hustle never stopped. One hand was always greasing the other. That's what made the world go around. We were living in the times of buy, sell and trade.

"Cool, you know I ain't trippin'. It's enough money to go around," she said, rubbing on my thigh as we pulled up to our destination. I didn't say nothing. "I hope you ready to break pockets and take names and numbers later, 'cause I am," she said, grabbing her purse once we were in park.

When we made it inside there were more people than I expected. Empty bottles were scattered throughout the room. People were making out in different sections and the other drinking, smoking weed, and playing craps. Music blasted through the speakers and I couldn't hear myself think. Just my type of environment. Mo' money, mo' problems, but I can handle myself.

"Y'all took forever. We thought y'all chicken heads wasn't coming," one of Zane's homeboys said.

"Boy, please. Where there's money to be made, there's the two of us," One said while we made a beeline to the bathroom.

By the time we made it there, two people came out almost knocking us down. "Watch it," one of them said as we slid inside.

"Bitch, you watch it," I said to the hoe while One checked the nigga.

"You got that's right! Watch my ass. They had better be thankful I don't want to blow my high. Come on, Cache." She grabbed my hand and I was grateful for that. I didn't feel like fighting tonight. My hair and nails were too fresh for all that. When we usually fought it almost always started because of One. "Here." She passed me a bump.

I got in position and did me. I snorted that shit up my nose like a vacuum cleaner. "Girl, what the hell are you doing?" I asked, looking over at One.

She had taken a cooker out with a half of a gram of H and cooked it. She then filled a needle with the liquid. *When had this hoe started fucking with the needle?*

"Girl, I can't just mess with that coke no more. I need a lil' Brown with it, baby. You'll see. Snortin' no longer gets me high. This shit here, though? One and one, I fucks with. You just haven't reached this part of the game yet," she said, still focused on the task at hand.

I didn't say nothing though because who am I to judge? The only difference is that we chose two different highs. I left well enough alone. I couldn't help but wonder how the hell did she start fucking with this shit. Did she know how dangerous it was?

“Don't trip I got this. I'm doing the safety thing, okay?” she answered the questionable look that must have been apparently written on my face. This answered a lot of my questions, too. Actions spoke louder than words. “Besides, I’m going to this clinic called The Needle Exchange. You’ll be surprised how safe this shit is.”

“What you mean safe?” I asked not knowing what she meant because there is no way there is a clinic that allows you to do dope. This Needle Exchange had to be some underground crap. Maybe a cut? “I wouldn’t trust the shit. It sounds like a setup. We both also know people who have OD-ed on this shit!” I shouted.

“It’s nothing like that, Cache. At The Needle Exchange, you have to be eighteen or older. You’ll get a needle kit with ten needles, rigs, cotton, a tie-off—let me see.” She started digging into her purse. She came out with the little kit. “Okay, we have alcohol pads, a cooker, and as for OD-ing, I got Narcan. So, if that ever happens, just shoot this in my thigh.”

“You gotta pay for that?” I asked curiously.

“Nah, it’s all free. It’s supposed to prevent exposure to Hep-C, HIV/AIDS. You get condoms also. I know I live my life on the wild side but I’m too young and sexy to die, especially from a nigga giving me a House in Virginia. No way.”

This shit explains why she losing weight.

“To me, it seems this exchange place is all a setup. Like, on some stuff, they’re saying it’s okay to kill ya self, but just be careful with spreading whatever it is you’ve contracted while killing ya self.”

“Okay, now that you say it like that, I guess I never looked at it like that. I’ll never share a needle anyway. Besides, you are the only one that knows my secret.” As soon as she said that, we heard someone banging on the door. We jumped.

“Mane, what y’all doing? The party out here!” Zane yelled, beating the door down.

“Boy, wait! You can’t rush perfection! Damn!” I yelled still, feeling a little salty towards him. I couldn’t believe he showed a different side to himself tonight. That’s exactly why I vowed to never let no one own my heart. Dudes are straight disrespectful when it comes to a woman's heart, including their own momma.

"Ain't nothing perfect 'bout y'all hoes! Now, hurry up before you lose out on ya' money!" He must've walked off because as soon as I slung the door open Ryleigh was standing right there.

"What?" I yelled, frustrated, placing my hands on my hip.

"Y'all, not the only ones got to use the bathroom," she said, looking behind me to see what we were doing.

I closed the door some. I didn't need her all in our business. "We'll be out. Give us five more minutes."

"Mane," she said.

I smiled politely before I slammed the door in her face, not giving her time to finish.

Twenty minutes later, we emerged from the bathroom, ready to get the real party started. We had both freshened up and changed into different outfits. One had on a two-piece pink Victoria's Secret set with a sheer white robe and a pair of pink Jimmy Choo heels. I had on a black, leather strap, one-piece with strappy, black leather Gucci heels that matched. Everything was exposed. My ass and breasts had yet to start experiencing the effects of gravity so they stood at attention and demanded respect when I stepped into a room. My body was coated with scented body oil. I didn't have any makeup on. Just a splash of Mac gloss covered my lips and my Cambodian hair flowed down my back. I've always been praised for my natural beauty on many occasions.

One and I had already decided that she'd dance first, and I would go last. "Save the best for last because if your big, fine ass goes first, they'll be running me off the pole like Sandman do on the Apollo." We shared a laugh.

I worked the floor and gave a few lap dances while she danced to *Undecided by Chris Brown*. "What's your name, daddy?" I asked, twirling my hips on his pole. The nigga had potential.

"Knowledge," he simply said without further conversation. His face was one I had never seen before so of course, I was curious to know why.

"I like that. Where you from?" I asked trying to keep the convo flowing. I was definitely attracted to this man but knew he would never go for a girl like me. Why would he?

"Thanks. And I'm from BR. Why? You don't mess with country niggas?" He smiled a dimpled smile and I started blushing.

"Nah, not at all. I'm not as predictable as you're making it seem," I said, flinging my hair at him sassily, letting him know he would have to come more correctly than that to figure me out. I didn't need him knowing I was also a country girl.

"What's your name, parenthesis?" he asked, referring to my legs.

"Nah, it's actually Cache, but everyone knows me as Beautiful," I said being funny.

"Oh, it's like that, huh?"

"I guess," I told him. It was time for me to go, so after the song was done, I told him I'd see him later. I kissed him on his cheek, and he stuffed the money in one of my many straps.

Before I could walk off, he called me back. "Wait." I turned to him. "How you know that?"

"Know what?" I asked.

"That you'd see me again?"

"I don't know. You tell me."

"Give me ya' number, ma."

I let these niggas pick their own destruction, but I also knew I had him at hello. Just as well as he had me. After giving him my number, I decided I would like to see him again, but under different circumstances. For now, I'll keep him my little secret. Something inside told me, there was something about him that I couldn't figure out. I felt something I couldn't explain. The nigga def had my mind wandering and that was something new to me. I didn't know if telling One was the right thing to do especially after the shit she pulled.

I made a mental note that we needed to have a come to Jesus meeting. I mean the crazy hoe was dawg and all, but I was not doing forty to life all because of a dollar.

After I left, I went to the DJ booth and requested a song change. I danced to *Work Me Slow by Xscape*. As soon as the beat dropped, we made eye contact and everyone else in the room wasn't there anymore. It was just him and me. I don't know why I was feeling this man as much I was, but I was. Money started raining on the stage, but not even that made me break eye contact with him.

"He's just a trick," is what ran through my mind. There could never be nothing between us, but something deep inside me longed for him. I continued to work the pole, converting back to what I came here for. That bag!

The song was ending but I wasn't ready for it to be over. It was apparent that the crowd didn't either so when the song switched over to *Maxwell's Woman's Worth*, I continued to do me. At the top of the pole, I slid down slowly, looking like a ballerina, ending in a split. Even with the music playing, I could hear my ass slapping against the floor. I looked around the room for One to get her approval, but I didn't see her nowhere in the weed smoke-filled room.

She probably giving someone a private dance. Ain't no telling with that girl. I smiled to myself, shaking my head at her.

She'd always been about the coins, no matter what it took to get them. When I looked back up to see if I could spot Knowledge, he was looking at me with hate on his face. I brushed it off, just figuring it had to be too many drinks. He slammed his drink and stormed to the back. I didn't know what his problem was, but I wasn't about to waste my time and find out either. Fuck 'em. One nigga didn't stop the show when you was in a room surrounded by niggas that pockets were deeper than the next.

***

One

This is where the real party at, fuck all that other shit. That shit out there didn't count when it comes down to doing dope. That's exactly why I decided to duck off in here away from everyone. I loved getting high because every time I shot up, the result would be cumming on myself. I have not had a nigga yet to fuck me as powerful as this shit. I definitely didn't need a man to do it for me. Plus,

I made my own money. I like to fuck around every once in a while, but to be honest, fuck a nigga! Money over everything! I didn't want to admit it to Cache, but the only thing that could change my mind about doing me was if there was something else better than this. I doubt that shit, though.

As I'm sitting there, slobbering from the mouth, enjoying myself and experiencing orgasm after orgasm, someone walks in. When I look up, it's Zane and he looks extremely angry. He's walking back and forth, drunk and talking to himself. I try to pull myself together as best as I could but I'm still kind of hazy. I instantly started laughing and I don't know why.

"Bitch, what the fuck you laughing at, huh?" he asked, looking at me with a demonic stare.

"Nigga, you," I barely got my words out before he started attacking me. "Get the fuck off me!" I screamed as loud as I could, but I knew that my voice fell on deaf ears.

"Hoe, you don't find nothing funny, now do you, Cache?"

What the fuck? Cache? This nigga was crazy. I kicked, scratched and punched with everything I had from the bottom of my soul. "Help! Stop! Get the fuck off me!" I instantly shook back and was no longer high when I realized what was happening. He was raping me and there wasn't anything I could do. Again, with all my might, I kneed him in his privates. I hated when a nigga did shit like this. Didn't niggas know you never have to rape a hoe?

"Bitch, calm the down!" he screamed, punching me dead in the face. "You hoes need to know how to stay in your place, but I'm 'bout to teach you a fucking lesson," I heard every word he was saying but didn't understand where all his anger was coming from.

To be honest, I really didn't care. All I knew was I prayed that he would hurry up and get it over with. That last punch had knocked everything else I had inside of me that quick. There was nothing left. The only thing I could do was pray a prayer of God's protection. Something that I had never done but was taught by the woman who raised me. Once he ripped me out of my clothes, he pushed himself inside my back door, mercilessly ripping me open. He pumped inside of me, grunting, sweating and calling Cache's name until he came long and hard. He took a minute, catching his breath. When he did, he stood up. Before pulling his pants up he grabbed my Victoria's that he ripped off me and used them to clean himself off.

"I know you will only allow adversity in my life to strengthen me. Therefore, I will accept any test that comes but I do not have to be defeated by the enemy," As my prayer was coming to an end Zane walked to the door.

"Ayo, my nigga come through!" he shouted through the door.

The next face that came in had me ready to commit suicide. I'd rather go to hell than for him to fuck me. My prayers must not have made it God because if they had no way would he let this shit happen. The smirk on his evil ass face was the last thing I saw before I blacked out.

CHAPTER 9

One Year Later

CACHE

It seemed like forever since I heard from One. I missed her dearly. Not so much as for the things we were into, but above all, I know she loved me. Despite the drugs, she had truly been a friend. That night at the after-party where we went to strip had turned into a disaster. One had been raped by Zane and one of his boys until she was unconscious. When I found her, she had been badly beaten and even urinated and spat on. They left her for dead. Knowledge and I had to rush her to the emergency room where she had been taken straight to the operating table.

After hours of waiting for the prognosis, the doctor finally came out with some good and bad news. "We were able to reconstruct her vaginal area and also her rectum. Over time she will physically heal tremendously. As for her mental, I cannot tell you where she will be. Just know she is a strong girl and we are praying for a full recovery."

I prayed and stayed by her side every day until she came out of her comatose sleep a week later. When she woke up and took in her surroundings, it crushed my heart that she put me out of her room. I just figured she needed time to take in everything that had happened to her, I was wrong. That had been the last day I saw or heard anything from her. I didn't know if she didn't want to see me because of shame or what. All I knew was that it hurt, and I missed her dearly. I tried understanding, though I knew I didn't hurt as much as she did.

Since then I had kind of changed my life around. I started wanting better and so that made me do better. I no longer worked anywhere around a strip club or any of the other things I was into. I went back to school, got my GED/HI-SET and no longer did drugs. I had heard through the streets that One was doing her thing, too, but she had gone a much different route than I. She no longer did drugs and she let all her tricks go. I heard she had found her *God*—she finally found a nigga on set to make it rain. I wish I could tell her how proud I am of her. I mean, her hustle will never change but I'm glad she put the drugs down.

As for me and my nigga, that night everything happened, Knowledge and I somehow grew stronger. Since then, we have been inseparable. I guess him seeing what happened to One messed his head up and made him want to play Captain Save A Hoe. I guess the saying, *"You can't turn a hoe into a housewife"* has been proven to be false. We've been kicking it like Bonnie and Clyde without causing havoc. I no longer looked at him as a target but as my savior. He brought me out of a place I never wanted to revisit. Thanks to him I love my life. I wouldn't trade it in for the world. I would do everything over again just as long as I could be in the presence of real love. Some say it's hard to find but I know from experience you will never have to find it because when it's real it will find you instead. Knowledge always jokes and says how love just fell into his lap, literally.

"Ayo, bae, you almost ready?" he asked me through the door.

"Yeah, give me a minute please," I said, whining because of the size 8 I tried on. The problem was me not being able to even squeeze inside this damn dress. "Baeeeee," I cried.

"Yeah?" he answered.

"I'm getting too fat. I can't even fit in any of my clothes!" I yelled through the door.

"You got other clothes. Some with tags still on 'em. You already know I don't care what you put on and neither will my parents. I prefer you naked." I could tell he was smiling through his words.

"Oh, you do, huh?" I joked with him, stepping out of the bathroom with my full body on display. "Well, show me how much you prefer it." I smiled at him sexually without any more talking. We communicated with body language. I wrapped my arms firmly around his neck, kissing him deeply.

He grabbed my breasts, slightly pinching my nipples. He knew what turned me on. "Think we got time for a quickie?"

"Make time," I told him and that's exactly what he did.

He fucked me and made me cum back to back. I could barely hold myself up. I was so weak. "Dang, King! I definitely might be having your baby after what you just did to me!" I smiled wanting more. He had woken up the beast inside me and my head was still spinning.

"Oh, yeah, that's how you feel?" he asked, gazing into my eyes. "So, if you were, would you carry my seed? My last name?"

"Fucking right. You know there is no King without a Queen. I love you, and to be honest, I can see us together forever."

I kissed him and we both started getting lost in each other again.

"We need to go, bae, before we really be late," he said, and I could feel his pole rising, ready for some more.

"You right, let's go. I'll take care of him on the road," I said, grabbing his dick.

***

We stayed in Denham Springs which wasn't far from where we were going. When we made it to Baton Rouge, my nervousness kicked in overdrive. This would be my first time meeting the parents. The whole time I have been hoping and praying that they'd love me just as much as he did. It's hard for me to be confident when it comes down to shit like this. I mean I'm not the type of bitch you bring home to momma, but neither was Cardi B and look at her now.

"It's alright, they will love you, I promise." He touched my leg, trying to reassure me that everything would go smoothly.

Even though I had never been through the whole meet and greet thing with parents I knew they would want the perfect mate for their child. In addition to him being the perfect gentleman, he had his own money, and I just hoped they didn't look at me as a gold digger.

At the moment I am unemployed, but I gave up my cashflow for my fairytale. After obtaining my GED I decided that I wanted to get some kind of job training skills. Even though Knowledge preferred me not to work, I still wanted to bring something to the table.

"We can't live off drug money forever," would be my response every time we had a conversation about me finding a job.

More than that, I felt that if he could get it together, I could, too. Six months ago, he told me to give him six months to hustle and he was out for good. I still don't think he's ready for all that. This some shit he been doing all his life. Taking his hustle away would be like taking away the air he breathes. He knew that I accepted him hustling and all, but I guess he wanted to show me life had more to it than what I have always been used to. Until that time comes when he truly is ready to let it all go, I'll be right here.

When we pulled up to this big, beautiful home right outside of Baton Rouge, I was in awe. It was in a town called Prairieville. I have heard about this place but had never been here. Too many white folks for my ass.

"We're here," he said. Knowledge hopped out to come open my door as he had done plenty of times before. I accepted his hand like I always do, and we proceeded to his mother's home.

"Welcome," a beautiful woman greeted us. She stepped out to the side for us to gain access. I wondered who she was, and I knew I did not want her around my man. I know I'm a sight for sore eyes but damn! I made a mental note to keep an eye on her at all times. I would hate to show her uppity ass how we do it in the south.

"What's up, ma?" Knowledge greeted her, surprising the hell out of me.

"Boy, don't what's up yo' mama. Naw, get in here and give me some suga." He kissed her on the cheek. "And you must be Cache," she said, welcoming me with a hug. "How are you, baby?"

"I'm fine. It's nice to meet you," I said, still amazed at how beautiful she is. I couldn't help but blush. She was the real definition of *black don't crack.* That or either she had Knowledge at a very young age.

"Come, your father has been waiting on you."

We entered the kitchen and there was a layout of all sorts of soul food. Something I hadn't seen in a while. My stomach instantly started growling.

"I see someone is hungry. Let's eat. We can get to know one another at the dinner table. Oh, and you can tell me what y'all gone name this baby she pregnant with," his mom said, grabbing my hand.

"I'm not pregnant"

"Mmmmm," she said, looking at Knowledge like she knew something we didn't.

I just dismissed what she said, I wasn't having a baby. Maybe she was trying to let Knowledge know I'm a keeper. I do agree.

Knowledge's father stepped into the room and I didn't have to wonder if he was the man of the house. They were the reflection of one another. It was almost scary. He also looked as if he had stopped aging around 35. This family definitely stopped aging a long time ago.

Instantly I knew I not only loved Knowledge but just being in this family's presence made me love them and want more out of life. They all looked so happy and complete. To be honest, I didn't understand why Knowledge had turned to the streets, especially if he had everything right here. This did make me miss my family. Tomorrow I will drop by just to say hello.

CHAPTER 10

The next day I pulled up in front of MoMo C.W.'s house and was surprised to see Ann. *Damn, my mom looked so weak. Small.*

"Cache, where yo' ass been?"

"Ann, chill. I'm not a lil' kid no more. Now come give me a hug like you miss my ass," I said, hugging my mom. Being around Knowledge and his family made me realize how much my family meant to me. Our shit might not ever be perfect but at least we were still together.

"You know I'm just joking, chile. Do you have some money to give momma? I need to pay a few bills."

"Girl, you too funny. What bills you have? I see you still a crook," I said laughing at my mom who had always been more of a friend.

"Bitch, I got bills, and trust me when I say the apple, I see has not fallen far from the tree," she said seriously, checking out my new ride my man bought me.

"You must be proud," I told her. I went into my bag and broke her off. "I put a little extra in there, mom." I just hoped she did what needed to be done because I knew one of them *bills* she needed to pay was with the local dope boy. Regardless, I love her no matter what. I had to learn to put my feelings to the side. I couldn't live my own life when I tried to live hers too. "Where everybody at?" I asked. Usually, the streets would be loaded with motherfuckers. That's just how Evergreen and Spain was— always poppin'. It was summertime. You would think the heat would run everyone away, but it brought everyone out.

"Well, I don't know if yo' funny acting ass knows, but just a few days ago some dudes crept through and started shooting like they did on Boyz-N-Da Hood. You already know how it go down in the hood. Them dumb motherfuckers probably out retaliating instead of out here making this money. As for Momo C.W., you know how she do on Sundays. She packed the whole house up and they all went off to church."

"Well, what happened with you? She thought the church was going to burn down when you stepped inside the Lord's House?" I asked laughing because I already knew how Ann was coming.

"Girl, I wasn't feeling too hot this morning. It was horrible. Besides, I am the church. You better start reading the Holy Bible," she said, shaking her head.

"Ann, you stay sick more than a lil' bit. Yo' ass needs to be checked inside a hospital twenty-four-seven. I'ma see if we can turn Baton Rouge General into your home."

"Girl, please, I'll rest when I die and don't you start talking all that talk about going to no damn rehab. You know that shit only for them rich, white folk. They can't tell me shit I don't already know. The first step is admitting my ass. I know I'm a damn addict and I don't need a bunch of white bitches telling me that shit," she huffed. "I wouldn't give them my damn hard-earned cash. I'ma stop when it's time to go sit on my throne next to the Lord. Shit, he turned water into wine, so I know a little crack won't stop my glory ride."

"That's something you don't have to worry 'bout if it's money. Ma, I got you. I just want you well," I said taking in how small and sickly she looked. She wasn't her usual size. I mean, she'd always been a thick woman, but I could tell something was going on.

"Yeah, well, I'm as good as I'm going to get. Whatever it is that's wrong with me, only the Lord can see me through. Not no damned rehab. Shit, if you ask me, it's mo' drugs floating 'round there than the streets. Just not my drug of choice. Anyway, when am I gon' meet this nice man of yours? And don't pretend like he don't exist. You cannot be 'shamed of me all ya' life."

"Ma, I'll never be 'shamed of you, so chill with all that shit. I just know if I bring my nigga around, we'll both be broke fucking with yo' ass," I joked. She'll beg ya' ass right up a tree if you let her. I loved her though because she was all about Cache.

"I hear ya'. Now, take me to get some beer, a few scratch-offs, and some Churches.

That's exactly what I did, but not before placing money inside Momo C.W.'s mailbox, without letting Ann see of course.

CHAPTER 11

It had been two days since I met my in-laws and only yesterday that I spent time with Ann. I had such a great time. We ate, drank, and laughed. Knowledge had such a great relationship with his parents that I longed for. He told them everything including the lifestyle I once lead. My first thought was to be mad at him for not coming to me first, but the more comfortable and relaxed they made me feel I was okay with it. Our relationship was so perfect. He made me feel like my life was out of a movie. I trusted him with my soul, but I don't know why it was so hard for me to tell him the secret that only stayed with me and my family. Sometimes I even forgot.

I looked over at the clock on the nightstand and decided to get out of the bed. No need for me to be laid up all day. A woman's job was never done. Even if I wanted to sleep in, my wandering mind wouldn't allow me to. Yesterday when I went out to grab me some milk and personal items, I passed by the aisle that contained pregnancy tests. I don't know what made me do so, but I did. Maybe it was the fact I hadn't seen my cycle or maybe it was the excessive weight. I also had been feeling a little morning sickness, too. It took the cake though when Knowledge's mom called me out on it.

After peeing on the stick, I waited five minutes which to me felt like a lifetime. "Finally," I said, noticing that the test had two pink lines. "Damn! Where did I put the box?" I asked myself, realizing that I should've gotten the test that read, *pregnant or not pregnant.* I looked everywhere but couldn't find the box. Minute-by-minute I got frustrated so I did the next best thing, *Google*.

I pulled out my iPhone to search the test and its results. When they popped up on the screen, I dropped my phone like it was possessed. Pregnant is what the two pink lines meant. I hoped Knowledge was ready to be a father because I was definitely not having a fucking abortion. *How would I tell him?* I thought while contemplating my next move. "Fuck it! Just tell him. He loves you he accepts you, flaws and all. Plus, you didn't create this child by yourself," I said, coaching myself that I didn't do anything wrong.

When I walked out of the bathroom, he was still asleep, so I decided to cook breakfast first. Yeah, that is exactly what I would do. I am gonna go all out, giving him breakfast in bed. Just in case he needed to sit down, he would already be there. I tiptoed through the bedroom, making it to the kitchen and went to work. I knew my way around the kitchen like I invented cooking. Of course, I cooked his favorite scrambled eggs with cheese and bacon bits, buttery, creamy grits, toast with crispy bacon and a cup of freshly squeezed orange juice. Now it was time to face the music.

"Babe, get up," I said, rubbing his arm and placing kisses all over his face.

He looked up at me smiling. *Damn, I could get used to this*, I thought smiling back.

"I love waking up to your face." He kissed me on my lips.

"Me too, bae," I said nervously, handing him the tray with his breakfast.

My phone sat on the side of his toast. He picked it up. "You're pregnant?" he asked but I could not read his expression. He held his head down toward the phone.

"Yeah, baby, I am."

He looked up at me and that's when I came from behind my back with the actual test. His smile melted my heart. He looked as if he had hit the lottery. I guess in his own way he had. We both had. That morning neither one of us ate breakfast because we were breakfast to one another. We made love three times that morning. He touched every part of me, including my soul. This is when I realized that I wanted to spend the rest of my days with the man I truly loved. He had opened a part of me that made me trust, and that's something that was taken from me years ago.

"Hold up, babe. Let me get this," he said answering his phone. "Hello?" I tried listening, wondering who was interrupting our bonding time. "Yeah, I'll be there." He hung up.

I decided to wait and tell him about the child no one, but my family knew about. I was ready to be open with him and to my daughter, too, because she deserved the truth more than anyone.

***

Knowledge 9:45 p.m.

Finding out that Cache is pregnant has only encouraged me more to put this street shit behind me. I not only wanted to, but I needed to be here for my seed. One thing, my father has taught me is how to be a man. I have enough money to live and take care of a whole village. I had invested my money through this import-export company that was run overseas. So, I had millions flowing in. Tonight is the night that I'm passing the torch. I know my boy Jock been waiting to take over the kingdom and he is definitely the nigga to reign on these muthafuckas. I pulled up to the trap house, taking in the scene for the very last time.

***

Cache 10:00 p.m.

Tonight, I want to cater to my man, especially because I know once I get big and pregnant, I'm going to be good for nothing. I plan to fuck him every day until I can't anymore. I wanted to make this a night to remember so I made every effort to impress him. I cooked his favorite for the second time today. Garlic shrimp and pasta, with cheese Texas toast. I put the Merlot on ice for him, and for dessert, I am serving me on a platter with whipped cream. I couldn't help but smile at the thought of me turning his ass out. I dimmed the lights, pulled out the scented candles and laid rose petals throughout the house, including the tub. If I wasn't already pregnant, after tonight, I definitely would have been.

Knowledge 10:10 p.m.

"What's good, my nigga? I'm glad you could make it," he said, dapping me down.

I was glad to see my dude, really, I was. Tonight, I was graduating to retirement. Not too many could say that. "I know my calling was unexpected, but I just wanted to check in before me and my lady headed to the fight. I didn't expect you to want to meet and it would have been pointless to head all the way back to her spot when I was already close to here. Ya, feel me? I hope you don't mind?" Jock asked, knowing how I was when mixing business with pleasure.

I could see the pleading look in his face as if this chick was harmless. But a pretty face don't mean shit. I'll let it go for now. "Not at all," I said, really not feeling him bringing this chick here, but I'm out of the game so I'll just get this shit over with. No reason to cry over spilt milk.

"A'ight, with that said this my nigga Knowledge and my lady Maya."

"Nice meeting you," she said smiling holding her hand out to shake mine.

"Same here." I took her hand into mine, I noticed her grip was firm. "A'ight enough of that let's get down to business so we can all get back to our lives. I don't want to keep the lady waiting. I know how Cache can get when a nigga keeps her waiting. Make yourself comfortable, we'll be finished in a minute," I said looking towards her for the last time. I couldn't help but feel we'd met before.

She did look very familiar, but I kept that to myself. No need to trip. To be honest, nothing could take my joy of becoming a father. "Let me make a call right quick."

"No problem."

Cache
10:30 PM

While I started putting the finishing touches on my makeup, the phone started ringing. Expecting it to be Knowledge, I picked up without looking at the screen. "Hey, baby," I answered sexily.

"What's good, babe?" His voice brought a smile to my face.

"Nothing much. Just wanted to make sure I was making the right decision."

"Oh, yeah, and what's that?" He didn't answer right away. I could tell he was hesitant. "I'm listening."

"Are you really ready to be with me?" he asked.

"Of course. What kind of question is that? Don't ever doubt me," I said, feeling some type of way.

"Go to the nightstand on my side of the bed," he said, ignoring my question.

Without asking him why I did exactly as he said. When I open the drawer, I noticed several things. Only one thing caught my attention. I instantly started crying when I noticed what it was, I was looking for. Let me assure you they were tears of joy. A ring.

"Oh, my God," I said.

"Now tell me are you still down?" he asked, and I could tell he was smiling. "I just want to make sure because if you not, you can always reconsider. I just want to make sure this is what you want because I'm a tough nigga to put up with."

"Hold up, bae, let me record this." I hit record, ignoring his last statement. "Alright, I'm ready." Just in case this nigga had a change of heart I'll have this to remind him.

"Cache, will you marry me?"

"Yes, yes, yes!" I shouted, placing the ring on my finger.

"My nigga, she said—" *Boom! Boom! Boom!*

Before he could complete his sentence, I heard gunfire that stopped the beat of my heart. I could hear something in the background but couldn't tell what it was.

"Knowledge! Knowledge? Babe, please answer me, King!" I screamed, using the nickname I called him. The only thing I could hear through the phone was faint breathing. "Please, God, don't do this. I can't lose you. We can't lose you, baby," I said. Holding my stomach and falling to the floor, I started screaming like I was possessed.

He had just taken his last breath. I know because even though I'm still physically alive, spiritually I had taken my last breath right along with him. How could the best night of my life become the worst?

CHAPTER 12

7 months later

"On the count of three, I'm going to need you to push. One, two, three," Dr. Ayanna Temple said to me.

"I can't do it!" I yelled, angry because of all the pain I was in. "I need the fucking shot! Now!"

"It's too late for that, baby. We need you to push," Knowledge's mom coached me as she rubbed my hand.

I know I had to be squeezing the life out of it but I'm positive she wasn't concerned with the lack of circulation. Her main concern was her grandchild being healthy, bright-eyed and bushy-tailed.

"I—just—want my king!" I cried, knowing there was no way I could get what I wanted. I needed him. I couldn't eat or sleep.

I had become dependent on this man and never thought about what I would do without him. My life really was nonexistent. For the last few months, I cried myself to sleep every night. I had nightmares of Knowledge getting shot and killed. I tried not questioning God but where was He when Knowledge needed his protection? He was changing his life for the better and this is what he gets? He didn't deserve this, for heaven's sake!

This curse over my life I thought I had finally broken remained. I see it had just been lingering in the darkness, ready to attack like a thief in the night. Right when I felt safe and secure.

"Keep pushing, honey, you can do this. I see his head."

I had been in labor for 13 hours, I was physically tired. Hearing that he was right there gave me the strength that I needed to get through. I silently counted to three and gave one big, final push.

"Aaaggghhh!" Then there he was my bundle of joy. When I saw his face, all I could do was melt. "He looks just like his father." I looked up at the new grandparents while tears flowed freely down my face. This moment was bittersweet. Even for them, they'd lost a child while I gained a fatherless one.

"Yes, he does. What's his name?"

I had been so caught up in my feelings I hadn't realized I hadn't taken the time out to think of baby names. That was something we were supposed to do together. I thought about it for a minute. "Knasir, it means *the king*." I looked down at him, repeating the name under my breath and knew he was truly a king. It fit him so well.

After celebrating Knasir's arrival. Everyone started clearing out with promises to come check on us later. I had been transferred to another room, which was filled with gifts, flowers, and balloons. Since my baby had been taken to the nursery, I decided to open some of the gifts. The first box I grabbed was from my mother-in-law. She bought my baby an outfit that says, *I love mommy but I'm a daddy's boy*. I smiled but it made my eyes misty. I hated it that my son would never get the chance to meet his father. Who would teach him how to shoot a ball or become a man? I didn't need the streets showing him how to shoot a gun or how to become a gangster. I know Knowledge would want the best for him and I just hoped I could provide that. I was afraid and lonely. It hurt so badly. When I first gave Knowledge the news of us becoming parents, I never thought I would have to do this all on my own. All my hopes and dreams had died right along with him that day.

I can't do this on my own. I wasn't sure how I would do this. *I guess just take it one day at a time.*

I moved on to the next present. There was no name, only a card, and some Gucci baby loafers. I smiled because they reminded of Knowledge. I opened the card and began to read: *Forgiveness is found in the eye of the beholder, but peace is gained within the righteousness - One Love*

"Oh, my God!" I screamed.

On numerous occasions, I'd prayed and hoped that my friend could find it in her heart to somehow forgive me, not really understanding why I needed forgiveness, but I did. Maybe it was because of the fact she had always been here for me when the world turned its back on me. I couldn't even have her back when she really needed me, and I guess that's where real forgiveness came in. The things we were in someone was bound to get hurt. I'm just glad we're both here to speak on it. Now with everything going on, it's like history was repeating itself. I needed her and here she was as she had always been, I smiled. I wondered how she knew I was here. Maybe she had never forgotten about me after all.

***

Out of the blue, a feeling came over me. I realized I couldn't do this, this thing called life. What was the true meaning of it all when you can't be with the one you love? *What about the baby you just had?* I asked myself, scared to take ownership. I can never be responsible for another human. Without thinking, I got off the floor and went to the nightstand next to my bed. I looked back at the door before I opened the drawer to make sure the coast was clear. I know it looked as if I was doing something, I had no business. My heart started racing and my palms started to sweat.

I didn't have to think twice. I had really grabbed the bag of Coke and ran to the bathroom. I locked the door behind me, pressed my back against it and looked around the bathroom searching for a spot. I ended up between the bathtub and the toilet, ripping the bag open carefully if there was such a thing. I sprinkled enough Coke on the side of the tub. Without warning, I start the hole in one swift motion.

For a moment, I regretted what I had just done, but only for a moment. My head slowly started to spin, and all my regret floated out the window. Once I felt the drainage that I used to love, I started sweating. I felt my heart rate speed up without warning.

"Cache, what you doing?"

"What you mean?" I replied looking up at the crooked smile. "I'm living," I told Knowledge. "How did you get here? This is me, I'm in heaven?" I asked touching his face when he came closer to me. Damn this some good shit I thought still smiling, feeling like dude off How High.

"Nah ma, we not in heaven."

"I feel like I am."

"Why are you doing this? We have a son now. You need to be a mother to the person who needs you more than I ever will. You let him down, you let me down. You are stronger than this, love."

"Actually, I'm not. I figured it all out, King. I can't do this shit without you. You promised me we would do this shit together. You lied to me!" I started hollering uncontrollably. "This is me, King. This life is the life I was living because of you and now that you are gone, I cannot finish." I felt the tears coming.

"Promise me you will not go down this road." He held my hands and for the first time in a long time, I felt comfort.

"The only thing I promise you is to join you real soon."

"Someone is knocking. Go answer the door and tell me if it is still worth you keeping that promise."

Not wanting to leave his side, I still obeyed and got up to see who could be on the other side. Opening the door, I looked around and realized it was all a dream. I was still in the hospital bed with Knasir, now in my arms. Whatever meds I was on really had my ass tripping.

"Damn, I almost gave up on you, son." Even though that dream was all I needed to keep me going, I looked at my son and was still unsure of what our future held. However, with everything in me, I knew the devil would come knocking and I wasn't sure if I was strong enough not to open that door. One thing I knew for sure was that I was damn sure going to fight, it was worth it.

***

The next morning, I got up and to my surprise, *a pleasant surprise I must say* I was staring into the face of a ghost.

"Hey! What's good, girl? Long time no see." One stepped through the door looking like a goddess. She came close to me, kissing both cheeks. "I must have missed you. You look damn good like nothing has changed."

"What's up with you, girl?" I smiled, she looked good.

"Chilling and trying to get my cake up. I see you have had a baby and everything." She smiled.

"Well, I'm glad to hear that and to see that you're alright." For a few minutes, my words lingered alone in the air. "I hope I didn't make you uncomfortable."

"I've been good, so where is his father? Why are you here by yourself?" I hung my head. "What, what did I say wrong?" she asked, rushing to my bedside to comfort me.

"Nothing, his father was killed seven months ago," I said concentrating on my hands.

"Oh, I'm so sorry to hear that! What happened?" she asked concerned.

"The guy I met the night everything happened with you, we started seeing each other. We were supposed to get married. It all happened so fast. One minute he was on the phone and the next, I heard gunshots." I started crying not able to hold my tears any longer.

"Damn." She hung her head, too. "I'm sorry to hear that."

"It's okay," that was the only thing I could say but it wasn't okay.

"So, why are you here alone?"

"Girl, I sent everybody home yesterday. I needed some time alone. It was just too much, you know?"

"Yeah, actually I do." She must've remembered putting me out. We both laughed, remembering how she reacted to seeing me. "I just recently lost my man, too." She looked off in the distance as if she was remembering a touchy moment. "But you know me, I'm used to keeping my shit together," she said snapping out of her trance just as quickly as she went into it. Out of the two of us, she has always been the strongest. Even with her being as strong as titanium I could still see the damage. The eyes never lie. "Forgive me for my actions, I was just upset, girl."

"All forgiven but it's not needed because we were supposed to have each other's back."

"Girl, that shit was out of your hands. Just look at it this way, at least you got a son and found love."

"Yeah, I got a son, but I found, then lost love."

"When do you get released?"

"Today, I'm ready to get my ass out of this room. Bitch, the walls feel like they're closing in on me," I said while packing my stuff.

"We definitely 'bout to get you out of this pale ass room. Bitch, where is my baby? Because that's the only reason I am here in the first place to pick yo' ass up," she said half-joking. I just didn't know how to feel about her calling my baby hers.

"Girl, the nurse came by earlier to get him. He should be back in a minute." Just as I said that my sisters and brother came through the door.

"Yeah, yeah. Give me the damn bags so we can hurry up out this bitch. I haven't even been here ten minutes and these mutha-fuckin' walls are closing in on me, too. Oh, I know you love my gift."

"Yes, I did." I smiled. "Thanks."

"Let me through this bitch," My ghetto ass sister Chanel came through the door like a true Baton Rouge Louisianan as One stepped out.

"Hey sis," my brother said, kissing my cheek giving me some flowers and balloons. A true gentleman the total opposite of his twin Chanel.

"Sorry, we couldn't make it for the delivery."

"That's okay. I didn't mind the time alone."

A'nett came and jumped in the bed to lay on the side of me like she did when we were kids. "Sup with you, baby girl? You been staying away from them knuckleheads?" I asked, looking down at her.

"No, her lil' fast ass gon' make me bust her and them and lil niggas up. I swear I'ma be getting life behind her," my brother said before A'nett could respond. He always felt that he had to be the man of the house.

"He's lying, sis." She gave me them puppy dog eyes that melted my heart.

"He better be, because if he's not I'ma be the one bustin' first. Fuck whatever happens later." She was growing up so fast and even though I had a smirk on my face I needed her lil ass to know I was serious.

"So, where is my nephew? That's who we came to see," Chanel said changing the subject. She had a soft spot for A'nett like we all did, but I'll be damned if I let these vicious ass lil' boys corrupt her.

"Damn, if one mo' muthafucka come in this bitch so boldly like I don't have no one in the world who care about me, I'ma go clean the fuck off," I joked, but damn.

"It's not like that, sis, niggas be busy just like you," my brother said.

I scrunched up my face as if I was saying *nigga, please*. I made a mental note to check his ass on that later. The streets talked and from what I hear, my brother was pushing dope. I didn't want that for him that's one reason I fucked, sucked and stuck a nigga up, so that they wouldn't have to. Later me and him would have to have a come to Jesus meeting. For now, I'll leave it alone.

"A'ight, I respect that." I shook my head acknowledging his words. "The baby is in the nursery though, Chanel." For a little while longer we talked before Chanel had to leave and go to work.

After getting everything packed up, One made her last trip to the car. I took a seat on the hospital bed and waited for the doctor to bring me my discharge papers to sign. As I sat there in my thoughts, I thought about One and everything we have been through. On the night I met the man I thought I would spend the rest of my life with, my friend was taken away. Now that my man is gone, she was here once again, like she always was.

Dr. Ayanna Temple stepped into the room covered from head to toe. The hijab didn't take away her beauty or from her personality. Her round face and doe shaped eyes told a story within itself. I guess beauty didn't come in the form of worldly things but from the beholder, a home where designer things didn't speak for you. A place where men respect their woman. I just couldn't get with my nigga having more than one hoe. Muslim people were lovers except when it came to war. They stood up for what they believed in, Unity, even if it was only for their own kind. Black people were only out for self, even in the beginning. You would think they would strike on the others, and towards their own kind show love.

I'm now in my twenties and still haven't heard my mother associate any of her words with love. One thing I promise is to not deprive and not express my love for my child. He will know that no matter what, he was conceived through love and that mine and his father's love ran deeper than the ocean. That only made me think of my baby girl.

"How are you feeling?" Dr. Temple asked.

"I'm okay, a little nervous about motherhood. Especially doing this all on my own," I said, comfortable in her presence.

"Don't be." She comforted. "One thing I can assure you is that motherhood may not come with instruction packages, but thankfully it comes naturally. You should have seen me my first time. God, I was a wrecking ball. After my second child, I knew I could do this with my eyes closed." She smiled, putting me at ease but I still pray she was right. "Anyway, I need you to sign these papers for me." She handed me the papers.

"Where do I sign?" I asked ready to bounce, a little more confident about this motherhood thing.

"Here and here." She pointed to the dotted lines. "I'ma go make copies of the release form and I'm also sending you home with two prescriptions, one for pain and the other for anxiety." After giving her the signed papers, she stepped out of the door as soon as One and Knasir stepped in.

"Girl, this baby is H.O.T! A real hot boy just like his father. Just to let you know I'm calling dibs."

"And I'm sending yo' ass straight to jail. Now give me my damn baby," I said laughing but also extending my arms to get him. I don't remember her ever meeting Knowledge, but she could have, so I didn't put much thought into it.

"Girl, not for me, I'm talking 'bout whenever I have my baby girl. Just know who he for with his pretty Italian looking ass."

"Bitch, you crazy. Let yo' child give her thang up to who she wants, too. Dang!" I laughed at her.

"Girl, if she anything like me and let's pray she's not, I promise you her ass ain't gon' be worried about nothing but Benjamins."

"Who is that?" I asked, lost.

"Sho' ain't the fuck, not Button! That money bag, Franklin! My name is not One for nothing," she said brushing her right hand across her left like she was making it rain.

"Speaking of, have you been thinking about your future? You gotta get back to the money while you been playing house, bitch."

"If you speaking of going back to where we started I'm out. Don't count me in, I'ma try the mother thing." I smiled.

"Girl, you know I'm just worried about your well-being. I know with ya nigga gone it's going to be hard to scrape up coins. You know we used to bring the house down. All the hoes used to be envious of us. Everyone hates to see us coming."

"Girl, for real? And here I thought I was liked by all."

"Bitch please, in my Deanna voice. Hoe, you had bitches waiting on child support checks to tighten up their inches. You know we fuck the game up wherever we go."

A knock came and in walked Dr. Temple with my papers and a nurse tailing her with a wheelchair.

"Okay, here we go. This is a copy of your release papers and I wrote your prescription for Percocet and Lorazepam. There is a possibility that you will be a little sore. If so, take this."

"Cache, handle your business. I'll be back. I'm going to grab the whip." One rushed out making herself useful.

When One was out of sight, she continued to talk, "I'm so glad she stepped out the room," Dr. Temple said. "I know not even a year ago, you lost your husband. I overheard your family speaking in hushed tones," she explained noticing the look on my face. She pulled out a business card. "I want you to take this. If there is anything I can ever do, I want you to call me and I'm coming. I don't know what it is but something about your story has pulled my heartstrings."

I accepted the card, placing it inside my purse. "Just know I have been in those same shoes and I can assure you it may hurt, and it may be hard but trust me when I say it is not the end."

I wiped my tears before they could escape my eyes. The nurse wheeled me out of the room leaving me hopeful and hopeless at the same time if that made any sense. When I made it outside, the sun was beaming down on us so brightly I couldn't help but smile and wonder if Knowledge was watching over us. One was at the door waiting for me. She looked good in her all-white Audi. I could tell she had done good for herself, I wasn't mad at her either. I hopped in her ride with a smile, happy to see my old friend.

CHAPTER 13

ONE

After dropping Cache and the baby off, I made a trip to the pharmacy to fill her meds. I didn't have to wait long because my girl Draya worked there. I was glad to be here for Cache. For one, it has been almost two years since me and Cache had any contact. The last time we had seen each other, we were hustling at this after-party in New Orleans that left me hanging onto life by a string. I used to hold her accountable for what happened to me that night. She should've been there for me is what I thought. We were always supposed to be each other *sister's keeper*. Especially fucking 'round in the game. Of course, that made me a lil salty. Any other time, she would've been on her shit, but she was trying to get wifed up by that nigga Knowledge but that's the past. I mean there was no beef, but we just didn't have that bond like we used to.

I must admit Cache didn't look the same. That spark that used to twinkle in her eyes was long gone. Even though she still had a body of a vixen, just having a baby and all, she looked terrible and seemed depressed. It broke my heart because kinda in a way, I felt I was the cause of some of that depression. That's why I'm trying to start by repairing what we once had.

"Here is your prescription, girl. So, what's been up with you Maya? Long time no see," she called me by my mother's given, I hated that name. She was absolutely the only person that called me that, Maya was long dead.

"Girl, I just been chillin' with my girl Cache. She just had a baby, so I came through to pick this up for her. It's good to see you too, though," I said, not really interested in the conversation.

"Oh, okay, so you have a family now?" she asked assuming Cache was my *girl* and also checking my temp. Not too many people knew I got down but the ones that did know would assume just like she did.

"No, at least not yet anyway." I smiled not believing I had said those words aloud. To be honest from that first day we met I was feeling Cache. That was the only reason I didn't leave her high and dry the day we hit our first lick.

"Oh, okay," she responded, shocked at my forwardness.

"Alright, I'll catch up with you later." Not really wanting to talk, I was on a mission.

"Cool, let's exchange numbers." She whipped her phone out without thinking twice. I did the same because she might come in handy.

After leaving Walgreens, I dropped Cache the meds and proceeded with the list of my things to do. I was headed to New Orleans. I needed to surprise Zane with a visit. I let the nigga think he and his homeboy had gotten away with rape. I refused to let them niggas think that shit was okay. I planned to show both of those fools they fucked over the wrong bitch. Since I didn't stay in New Orleans, I decided to get a room at the Marriott on Canal. I had people I could have gone to drop in on, but I was trying to be as low key as possible. I didn't need my face plastered over The First 48.

I needed to relax I felt so uptight. For the last few months, things had been so stressful for me. Little by little I was relaxing that stress by crossing the names on my shit list off. When the rape happened, it did something to me. It changed me so I made a promise to myself. If it was the last thing I do before closing my eyes I will get back at everyone that caused me pain. For the moment though I'll take a philly and roll me a blunt with a shot of Patron. After lighting, then inhaling, I decided to turn on the TV to surf through the channels. That shit didn't last long, I'm always easily distracted. The only thing on my mind was getting at that nigga Zane tonight. Knowing that in a few hours I'll be doing exactly that the thought made me cream. Without much more contemplating, my manicured fingers slid down into my shorts. There was nothing like bustin' a nut right before bustin' a nigga's head.

Strip Clubs

I was already on top of the costume that I will be wearing from Hustler Hollywood. My nails, hair, and eyebrows were already done and as for my MAC makeup, it was done to perfection. I knew I was that bitch and to top my outfit off, I placed a mask over my face. It was like the ones they would wear to a ball or costume party to disguise my appearance.

I knew Zane's routine like the back of my hand, I'd been watching his ass for a while, so there was no problem catching up with dude. I was sure my plan would work, I just had to be on my shit and catch the nigga slipping. This had to be a touch and go. I couldn't mingle or be tied to the club. Only a few knew I was here, and they were solid and loyal to me. I hadn't shown my face around the place in a lil' minute so I def' didn't need to be seen before or after.

Around midnight, like clockwork, Zane's sorry ass strolled into the joint like he was running shit. From the looks of things, it seemed as if the nigga had hit the lottery. I couldn't believe this fool had the nerve to walk around here like he's King Tut or some shit. Word around the club was his punk ass was that nigga, but this shit he was doing didn't make him a man. He didn't have respect but used intimidation to place fear in the hearts of these losers. After tonight we'll see if his bitch ass would continue to rape and beat bitches for fun.

As I continued to watch the nigga from afar, I had to laugh because he had no clue he was living on borrowed time. I checked the nigga out on side of him, but I couldn't see his face. The snapback was pulled down too far blocking my view. How was I going to get this nigga by himself? I guess I'll just have to come up with something tonight is definitely his last night on earth. I had already let this nigga breathe the same air as me for long enough. The only way this shit wasn't happening would be if God came down and saved the nigga. Other than that, this nigga's life had been written in stone.

Low and fucking behold! Guess who was with the nigga, following him just like a fucking dog? The nigga that played a part in raping me. Instantly my trigger finger started itching but this wasn't the time or place to turn this bitch into a bloody massacre.

"Damn, this had to be my lucky day," I said to myself smiling.

I could feel the thong I had on getting moist in the seat. I needed to get these niggas alone and the only way to do so was to invite them to the Velvet Room. I just had to grease a couple of the right hands. That wouldn't be hard for me to do, though, because money talks and bullshit walks. I made sure I paid a waitress to send the nigga an invite. I also broke the nigga Big Mike off a lil' extra for the Velvet Room. Now, all I needed to do was wait.

CHAPTER 14

ZANE

Bypassing a bouncer is something I never had a problem with. I was well respected and known around here, this place was like my second home. Besides pushing pills and weed, I recruited a few girls, placing them hoes on my payroll. It took me a lil' minute to learn but I got it now. You def' could not turn a hoe into a housewife. I decided to go with my move, though. Fuck being Mr. Nice Guy. As that saying go, if you can't beat them join them. I fucked the game up when I stopped treating these hoes with respect. All I did was stop trying to save these hoes and continued doing what every other nigga was out here doing, becoming daddy.

Women didn't want respect anymore, they loved when a nigga called them hoes and bitches. They loved when a nigga slapped them around and them hoes loved when a nigga took that cat. To a lot of these bitches, I was their savior and my hoes called me Black Jesus. I had to put the fear of God in them tricks. A couple of years ago, that hoe Cache had pushed me to the edge when she played me for that new nigga, Knowledge. Out of all the hoes I came in contact with there was something about her that I had to have. She didn't give in to me like everyone else. She always knew how to make a nigga feel like shit and I couldn't take it any longer.

That bitch played hard with a nigga, so when she agreed to come fuck with a nigga at the party, I thought I had her where I wanted her. But the bitch proved me wrong and decided to fuck with the next nigga with deeper pockets. Over time watching her every move, I developed a great deal of respect for her. For her, stripping was only a job, an act of survival. So, what gave a nigga like me the nuts to approach the situation? To this day, I still don't know. She made me lose all respect for women and had me feeling like less than a man. Something in my gut told me she was fucking that dike bitch, One. She was always cockblocking, shutting a nigga down like she owned Cache.

That night at the party, seeing the hoe Cache put on for that nigga Knowledge pissed me off. I stepped in one of the back rooms to cool off because the hoe had me fuming. At any moment I felt I was about to blow up like the World Trade Center. All it took was for that bitch One to laugh at me like I was Kevin Hart. I went straight off, I lost it. I didn't regret it though, because I put a lot of fear in the hearts of these hoes. They knew I wasn't the nigga to fuck with. Some might say what I do is bitch made, but how I see it, it's self-made, self-paid. Fuck a bitch.

"Black someone's tryna get down with the stable. She asked me to give you this note," Stormy, the waitress said when she approached with my usual nightcap. I had bitches come through all the time inviting me to the VIP section to show me what they were working with. I didn't give it a second thought.

"Cool, I'll be there after a while," I said as she walked off.

"You ready to go check this shit out, my nigga?" I asked looking over at my boy Mascot, my partner in crime. After that nigga kept it solid that night, I made him my right-hand man.

"Shit, yeah. You know I'm always ready to fuck with the hoes. This hoe better be bad and not waste a nigga time, know what I mean?" He laughed.

"Fucking right. The last bitch was fat, and we could've put the hoe on but when we stepped in the room. Lord, that hoe smelled like a lifetime of get back." I laughed, too, shaking my head. "Let's go handle our business."

"Big Mike, what's cracking?" I gave the nigga dap. He knew I didn't really fuck with him, but I tried keeping everything with everybody around here on the up and up. All the fat nigga did to respond was a head nod. *Whatever,* I thought as long as his faggot ass didn't get out of line. If so, Mascot didn't have a problem fucking him, too. *Hating ass nigga,* I thought before I stepped behind the door.

***

One

To my surprise, the nigga was at The Velvet Room sooner than expected. It was only like 1:35, which was perfect timing. His boy Mascot decided to come through, too. That shit was fine with me. I smiled and directed a waitress over and asked her to go to the DJ Booth in 30 minutes. I was requesting any song that I could shake my ass too. I really didn't give a fuck what it was, I just needed to get the job done. Just as I had that thought, the two guys stepped into the room. Lights, camera and action!

I grabbed the two by the hand, leading them exactly where I wanted them. I had everything they would need so there was no reason for them to leave the room. Hypnotic, Absolut and Moet chilled on ice. I fixed them glasses of whatever they wanted. As for me, I didn't need anything because my adrenaline kept me high. Just as I finished serving, a reggae song started to play. That was my cue, the perfect song. I slithered all over the stage, grinding, and humping like my life depended on it. My eyes behind the mask were fixed on Zane. He didn't take his eyes off me. He licked his lips while grabbing his dick. I knew I was doing my job. He continued to drink and that made my pussy wet. I knew without a doubt the nigga's clock was running out.

After the song ended, I went to change but not without letting him know to hold tight.

"I'll be back, Daddy," I whispered in his ear, running my tongue across his lobe. "Mission accomplished," I said, walking off while making sure the nigga saw my ass clap. Now that's what you call a round of applause.

***

Zane

Pimping ain't easy. That's what they say, but I beg to differ. There is no complication when it comes to making money. I tested my product before placing it on the market always encouraging my hoes to do that freaky shit. That'll keep the clients coming back and wanting more. Besides, pussy is power and will never go out of business. It is a proven fact that pussy will always be in supply and demand. Lawyers, judges and political figures and even the Pope like to fuck. It is a part of all walks of life, just like food and water muthafuckas just can't live without it.

I smiled because I loved my job, pimping ran like a line production and if my hoes got out of pocket, I never minded checking them bitches like Nike.

"My nigga, I hope this hoe know we both getting a sample of that pussy," Mascot said.

I ignored him, taking in my surroundings. Stormy, one of my bitches had gone all out with buckets of Hypnotic, Absolut, Moet, the bitch even had a few blunts for a nigga. To the average nigga, he would have been impressed but to Black Jesus, this is what would only be expected for a nigga like me.

"My nigga that hoe bad," Mascot said what I was already thinking.

"Yeah, she is. I got to have that bitch on my team," I said with my head feeling light. I must've had too much to drink.

"Fucking right," he agreed while passing the blunt to me.

"I'm back, Daddy. How you feeling?" she said, sneaking up on me. I didn't even notice she came back into the room.

"I'm good. So, what's ya name? Nigga def' need to put you down," I said, thinking she was bottom bitch material.

"Cake," she simply answered while rubbing my shoulders.

"Oh, yeah?" I smiled thinking of all the money the bitch could bring in.

"Yeah, I believe in letting a nigga have his cake and eat it, too."

I tried passing a blunt back to Mascot, but the nigga wouldn't take it. When I looked over to see what had the nigga attention, he was knocked out. From the corner of my eye, I saw the chick make a swift move. Before I could react, the bitch had a gun to my head.

"Bitch nigga don't fucking move!" she said. She removed her mask and my heart dropped to my ass.

"One!" My eyes damned near popped out my head when I realized too late who it was. "Muthafucka," I said, knowing I'd fucked up. Without being able to say my last prayer, she had pulled the trigger.

One

Now it was safe to say mission accomplished. After seeing that the shit I spiked the bottles with didn't knock the nigga Zane out, I had to move to plan B. I had hated for things to get messy but sometimes a girl's gotta do what a girls gotta do. Having everything said and done, I wasn't disappointed at all. Better them niggas than someone else. A nigga like Zane was bound to fuck up again and I just couldn't live with knowing the nigga was still breathing. Justice today had definitely been served. When the job was done, I slipped out the back door the same way I came in. Not before breaking my girl off something proper, though. I pulled my phone out to see if I had any missed calls. I didn't but I dialed Cache's number to see if she was still up.

"Hello?" she answered sounding like she had never been to sleep.

CHAPTER 15

CACHE

4:00 a.m.

I had just got up to feed my baby when One called. I had no clue what her ass could have been doing up at this time of morning, but I told her it was cool to come through. I needed the company anyway.

An hour and a half later, she was knocking on my door. Without peeking out the peephole, I just opened the door to let her in.

"Hey girl," she said while air kissing me. It was kinda cool outside, so I tightened the silk robe. I also noticed One's eyes fall to the opening of my robe. I didn't say anything, I just pretended I didn't notice her.

"What's up?" I said.

"Nothing just wanted to come back to help you out. I had a feeling you would be up with the baby."

"Yeah, girl his ass eats like a champ." We laughed.

"Babies do that. Anyway, I just had a few things to handle out of town. I hope you don't mind me dropping by this late."

"Nah, not at all. I was already up, and I do need the help." I smiled.

"Alright, I'ma hit the shower first, clean up and I will be there."

"Cool," I said, walking to my room to continue my motherly duties.

***

My six weeks had come and gone. One was still here helping me out. I was happy that she did decide to stay. Having her around, I had started feeling better about myself. All my baby fat was gone. My body was back to its old self, but even better. I still didn't know what I was going to do about money. All I did know was I wasn't feeling this shit. Being on welfare is out of the question. No way was I going to be one of those. I couldn't go back to school like I wanted to either. At the moment, the shit wasn't paying the bills. I needed to come up with a plan and quick. It's not like I never been on my ass and don't know the right moves to make because I did. Shit was just different for me now.

One been throwing me a few dollars, but the shit was getting old. She knew how I was so she would be slick by going to pay my bills without telling me. She would see something come in the mail from energy and before I could take care of it, she would already be on top of it. She even dropped money off in MoMo C.W.'s mailbox for me. Don't get me wrong, I wasn't complaining because a bitch needed the help, but I have always taken care of myself.

Life is crazy how one day you can not only feel but physically can be on top of the world, then everything comes crashing down. I guess that's why they say, *never say never* because you are only accountable for each second of your life. In a snap of a finger, everything could either change for better or worse.

"So, you want to do something tonight—celebrate?" One asked.

"Nah, not really. What would we be celebrating anyway?" I asked curious to know what she would say. I wasn't in the mood for all that.

"Fuck I don't know anything. Knasir is out of the house for the first time. You are free to be an adult. Fuck whatever you want," she said while lighting a blunt.

We went on the back patio because I would never smoke inside. Plus, I hadn't had any weed in a long ass time. My pain medication was out, and I had no refills. I had to medicate with something, right?

"I don't know, One. You know it's been a while since I been out. Besides, I could take this time to clean the house and get a few things done while Nas' is gone."

"Bitch we can call Mary's Cleaning Service for that shit. You know they got all kinda shit these muthafuckas out here doing for money."

She laughed, passing me the blunt. You know times have def' changed. One's ass never bought weed.

"I don't have money or nothing to wear."

"Girl, that's not an issue. I got you, you should already know that" she suggested.

"Mane, I don't know." I thought about it.

"Come on, C, I just really want to spend some time with you. I missed you—I missed us." I looked over at her ass enticing me with her puppy dog eyes.

"Alright, bitch! You get on my fucking nerves and yo' ass know you looking at me like that was gon' persuade me. Slick bitch." I rolled my eyes while passing the blunt back. "I gotta stop smoking this shit because this fucking my nails up. It's turning them bitches brown."

"Don't try to change the subject." She smiled while coming closer. "I'm glad to know that look influences you. What else would it entice you to do?" she asked all in my face, breathing in my air. She was only a few inches from my face. I couldn't help but look directly in her eyes. I placed my hand between the two of us letting her know I wasn't with the shit. My pussy betrayed me, though. It had a mind of its own. She looked at me with a questionable expression while running her hand up my thigh to see if I would object. Unfortunately, I didn't do shit. She then kissed my lips and again treachery overcame me. I loved the taste of her strawberry MAC lip gloss—I wanted more.

One, always being the aggressor, made me lay back in the lounge chair. "Kick ya slippers off."

She didn't have to tell me twice. She helped me slide out of my shorts next. I didn't have any panties on so that wasn't no problem. Good thing I had a wood fence surrounding the backyard because my legs were busted wide open. My pussy exposed while the sun shined on my flower, making my juices glisten and tell all my secrets.

"Damn you wet—just like I like it."

"Stop talking," I said, letting her know I was ready to be fucked. I needed it. From how my pussy was exposed, I could look down and see my clit swollen. The contraction was on the same beat as my heart.

"Give me a minute." She jogged inside, coming back out not even two minutes later with a sack in her hand. *The Fuck?* I didn't question her though.

She took her place back front and center diving in between my thighs showing me no mercy. This time was different. I craved what she had given me once before. Her touch had become foreign but not forgotten, if that made sense.

"Yesss," I moaned unwillingly but I couldn't help it.

"You like that?" she asked.

"Fucking right," I said running both my hands through my hair, pulling it slightly because I needed to grip something.

"Play with it for me. Let me see you cum," she demanded.

I did exactly what she asked. She took off her clothes. I did not know what she expected from me, but little did she know, this time I was open for whatever. That weed def' had a bitch lit. *That's some good shit*, I thought.

She came over and licked my cum off each finger. The shit turned me on so much.

"Can I taste you?" I asked without thinking about what I had just said. But looking at her body made me want to.

"You sure?" she asked.

If I really didn't want to do this now would have been my time to take it back, but I didn't. "Yes," I assured her. Like I said it had to be the weed.

She laid down in one of the lounge chairs that surrounded the pool. The kind you can lay down in with your legs up. I followed. Without a clue of what I was supposed to do, I just did what I thought and gave her what I would want. In no time, she was calling my name. I don't know if it was because I knew what I was doing or if she just enjoyed me. It wasn't bad at all and I must admit I enjoyed the taste. At first, I wasn't okay with it being slimy but the more I knew it felt good to her, the more it made my pussy wet.

In the sack she brought outside, I soon found out what was inside. A strap. Once she placed it on her, I was now on my knees waiting on her to pull my hair, slap my ass, while stroking the kitty. That's exactly what she did with no disappointment. Soon after, we both came but she was fucking me so good that I came a few times before we came the last time together. When all was said and done, we both had forgotten all about the plans we had made. For the rest of the night, we fucked some more and laid up.

CHAPTER 16

ONE

Good pussy was hard to come by. That was one of the reasons I decided to let that shit go between me and Cache. I knew the time would come when I would be able to slither my way right back between her thighs. I was just waiting until her six weeks were up. I always had a method to my madness. All my plans for us would soon be falling back to where we left off. A bitch like Cache was not easy to keep. She loved making her own money. Fuck, her name spoke for itself.

Soon we will be back hitting licks together and fucking the game up. At the rate shit used to be for us back in the day, we would have soon been touching millions. Fuck selling dope, pussy had the most power. It was and always will be phenomenal, exceptional, tangible. Muthafuckas can't deny that it ruled the universe. A nigga had to be crazy to think money ruled the world. Of course, it made the world go around but I had to agree with Beyoncé, girls are what ruled. Start from the beginning and you'll see Eve's shiesty ass made Adam bite the apple. Yeah, that shit always made me think of what apple they were referring to in the bible that had been so sinful that it changed the whole world.

Anywho, as I said, I planned to have shit back under control, very soon. I was glad to have put that beef behind me with Zane. Right game, wrong bitch. If the nigga thought he could ever run up on a bitch like me and all would be forgiven and forgotten, he surely knew what the fuck was up now. As for the case, the N.O.P.D had no suspects and no witness. That's just the way I liked it. Dead muthafuckas can't talk so everyone that played a part in Zane's dismissal was now flower pushing.

The other day when the shit went down between me and C, I never got the chance to take her out. Tonight, I planned to do just that. She deserved it, plus today is her birthday. Nothing had been established between us, but everything was cool. She wasn't looking for nothing and that was fine by me. As long as she wasn't fucking with these niggas, everything was good. Unless it was for a job, I can respect that shit. I been tricking off on C, making me feel just like these trick ass niggas out here. Money wasn't an issue though.

"Hello." I picked my phone up on the first ring expecting it to be Cache.

"What's up, baby girl?" she asked.

"Shit nothing, what's up with you?" I smiled happy to hear her voice. "I hope you ready for tonight."

"Fucking right. I hope you don't mind Reign tagging alone. She stopped by the house to see the baby and dropped off a gift for my B-day. She brought a bitch a fire ass Gucci bag and the heels to match."

Reign, the fuck?

"Oh, when y'all started hanging?" I asked feeling some type of way. Reign was this bitch we worked with back in the day. I didn't too much like or trust that bitch.

"We got tight since I stop working at the club. She been out of town for a lil' minute you know that girl can't stay out of trouble. She got a warrant out for her arrest and she had to bounce for a while. You know how it be."

"Yeah—I do." Not really feeling this hoe, fuck Reign

"Anyway, she rolling with us. I hope you really don't mind."

"Nah, I don't but look let me handle my lil' business. I'ma hit you back after I get done." I didn't even let her finish before I hung up. Tonight was supposed to be all about us, not no fucking Reign. That shit really pissed me off. She coulda asked first because I already know she told the hoe it was cool.

I pulled out a bag of coke and snorted a line right there in my car. I'd been stopped fucking with that H. That shit was the reason I was raped in the first place. Cache didn't know I was still fucking with this shit and I planned to keep it that way.

***

As always, me and Cache always shut shit down. To compliment her Gucci bag and pumps, she wore a white crop top with white jeans that fit her as if they'd been painted on. I'm not gon' lie I wanted to rip that shit off and fuck her in front of the crowd. From the first day we met, I saw something in her. I always knew she belonged to me. I chose to keep her for myself that day. She didn't know it but that day I saw something in her I had to have. I lived by the no witness, no case but that one time I had to break my number one rule. In the end, she was worth it. Tonight, whenever I felt the courage, I would let her know exactly how I felt.

Never have I been gullible or the awestruck type when it comes to beauty but there is something different about Cache. I just couldn't figure it out. Maybe it's me having Mommy issues which is something I'll never admit, or it could be the fact that I see so much of myself in her. Who knows? If I wasn't careful this bitch could have me in the palm of her hands. I just constantly remind myself that I can't save that lost girl inside of someone else. It's very hard abiding by my own rules. The question is—is she worth it? My answer, I don't know but time will reveal.

I watched as she and Reign danced together. I wasn't tripping on that shit because I knew where we stood. I had her exactly where I wanted her to be. I really wasn't feeling the shit, but I didn't want to show my jealous streak so for now, I'll chill. I do plan to keep a close eye on this bitch because something in my soul told me she was being a snake.

Cache

Every time I stepped into this club, it reminded me of the love of my life. Even though we met at the after-party, for some reason it reminded me of that night. It felt different stepping back in here. A lot had changed but then you also had shit that'll always be the same. Reign broke the news to me the other day that Zane got killed right here in this same club. The shit was crazy. She said that was one reason she had to get the fuck away. The cops kept harassing her. That's the shit they do when they try to get a bitch to talk. She wasn't willing to cooperate, so she got the fuck. It was really funny that One didn't hip a bitch to what had happened. That made me wonder if she knew. I made a mental note to run that shit by her. I didn't focus too much on it though because that dirty dick ass nigga deserved everything he got. No telling what happened. Maybe the nigga's shit caught up with him.

I was enjoying myself tonight. It really had been a minute since I got out and was able to find something to smile about. I missed Knowledge like a muthafucka but I know he wanted me to live my life and not be in the house ready to commit suicide. To be honest, what me and One had going on brought me a little happiness. I loved her fucking me, she helped me out with whatever I needed, and we were still able to put our friendship first. She understood me and knew where I've been and where I am now. Being with her didn't make me feel like I was cheating on Knowledge. I don't think I could ever find a man that could compare to him so, for now, I'll stick with what I know, One.

"Look what the cat has drug in." I turned around to the voice and was face to face with this blood-sucking bitch, Angel.

"Bitch don't start," I told her walking off because today wasn't the day to fuck with me. "Reign, fuck her, she not worth it," I said, realizing she was ready for Angel to get stupid. This time she walked off with me but before I could get far this bitch had the balls to grab me by the arm.

"Let me the fuck go before I go loco on yo' ass," I said speaking that hoe's language thinking that she would feel me, but the hoe's grip got tighter.

"The fuck going on over here?" One walked up ready to jump. "Get yo' fucking hands off her." One pushed Angel back.

"Oh—okay, I see. So, what, you fucking her now, too? Cache, she knows how to suck puss—"

Before Angel could get her words out, One had knocked them bitches right back down. I just knew some shit was about to pop off, but then again everyone knew not to fuck with One.

"Fuck you, One!" She spit blood out her mouth, almost touching my Gucci's.

"Let's go y'all. Fuck her," I said knowing security would be coming soon.

"Bitch you ain't no better than the next bitch in here. Just because you had a nigga come play captain save a hoe don't mean shit. Look where you had to come back to! Bitch, the nigga probably killed himself realizing he could never turn a hoe into a housewife."

I turned around swiftly and with everything in me, I came with it from the bottom of my soul. My spit landed straight across her face into her eye. This disgusting hoe wiped it off with her hand and licked it. I instantly got mad all over again. Maybe because my first attempt didn't faze the bitch. Without thinking, I grabbed a glass bottle by the neck, broke it, and went crazy on her face like I was Edward Scissorhands. The way I worked her loudmouth ass you would have thought the hoe was dead. She def didn't have shit else to say.

I must have blacked out because the next thing I know I woke up freezing cold in the Parish jail. I must have been a lil' drunk too because everything was foggy. I looked down at my clothes and I was soaked in Angel's blood. I was caught red-handed, literally. I had to get the fuck out of here, my baby! I should have been thinking about that shit from the jump, but I was just flashed. Fuck, I should have never let that hoe get under my skin. The realization of what I had done started to kick in. I had to call home. Why wasn't I already out of this place?

"Yo' who after you on the phone?" I asked the girl dialing the same number for the hundredth time. *Bitch, if they haven't picked up yet they don't want to.* Fuck! Of course, I kept that shit a thought. This hoe was at least six feet tall, the average height for a man, black as fuck and the bitch looks like she worked out. I could have placed my right hand on the Bible, testified in open court that the broad was def a man. That was until I noticed she was missing an Adam's Apple. Oh, and let me not forget the ruby red lipstick. In my book, she could def' pass as drag. I wouldn't have answered either if I were her people. Hell, I don't know how her momma had the courage to take her ass from the hospital when she was born. So again, those thoughts were kept safely to myself.

"You—but come on cuz, I'ma give him time. I don't know why he didn't pick up the fucking phone," she said angrily.

Instead of saying anything to her, I smiled politely and dialed One's number. I kept a close eye on she-man because even though she sounded all woman I still wasn't sure if this hoe would pull out a dick or not. Judging from her size 13 shoe, I know if she did, that bitch would be longer than my arm.

After dialing One for the second time, I hung up and just got back in the line. I could see these hoes looking crazy, but when Godzilla's ass had the phone for an hour, these bitches was twiddling their thumbs and finding dirt in their nails that only they could see. Scary hoes! I just let the shit be. I had bigger fish to fry. I don't know what the fuck is up with One. I made a mental note to get in that hoe's ass. If it wasn't for her and that bitch Angel having a past, I would not be in this fucked up predicament.

"Cache Price, intake," a C.O. came to the cell reading my name off a clipboard. I never been locked up, so I didn't know what intake was. It couldn't have been good, though. I just stood up, placing my hands through the gate so that I could be cuffed.

"Ayo—what's yo' name, ma?" someone screamed at me.

"Mane fuck him. Holla at a real nigga." I was nervous as fuck. Dudes were hollerin' from every cell block like they'd never seen a piece of pussy before. My outfit didn't make it any better either, but I just kept my head straight. You would think I would be used to this kinda thing, but I guess it is a whole different story. Money is the motivator and the equation.

"How are you, Miss—"

"Price," I said to the nurse.

"Yes, Miss Price. I'm going to work you up and then ask you a few questions.

"What you mean?" I asked not knowing what he meant by *work me up*. That shit sounded very sexual if you asked me.

"I'm going to check your vitals, temp, and pressure and weight. The normal thing you would do if you were to go to the doctor's office." He smiled.

"Oh, okay." Without further questions, I sat back and let him do him. After an hour of the intake process, the officer didn't waste any time taking me to the back. As soon as I made it to the pod, I went straight to the phone. Thank God I didn't have to wait.

"You not gon' get through." I heard someone say through the dark.

"What you mean?" I asked trying to figure out who was talking to me.

"The phone's off. You've got to wait till morning. If you caught trying to use the phone, you'll get locked up." I didn't need to hear anymore, I hung up the phone. Grabbing my mat and intake bag, I went into the living area and found an empty bunk. I knew it would a long fucking night.

CHAPTER 17

ONE

My head was hurting. I didn't expect none of that shit to pop off tonight. That hoe Angel had me wanting to kill her ass. If it wasn't for the bitch laid up in the hospital fighting for her life, she would be dead already. I can't lie, I feel like this shit is all my fucking fault. Of course, I didn't think me, and Cache would be where we are, and that hoe Angel would feel some type of way. No one knew what was going on between us but Angel being Angel, she was like a hound dog when it came to someone fucking her. No, I wasn't fucking her anymore, but I guess that was her fucking problem! I'ma fuck the bitch alright! Fuck her ass clean up if she pulls through.

I was trying to see how the fuck I was going to get Cache out of jail. I missed both of her calls. I been waiting on her to call back, but she never did. I made several calls to see what her bond was looking like but I kept hitting roadblocks and getting the runaround. Each time, I was told that she hadn't gotten processed yet. When she finally was booked in the parish, the shit turned to me waiting until the morning. She would go to court for a bond to be set and I planned to be there to post it. Waiting was exactly what I been doing, too. I couldn't even sleep, and it wasn't from the Coke. I knew she was going through it and I couldn't do shit about it.

"Fuck!" I shouted angry with the world. The only thing I could do as I waited for a bond, was roll a fat one. I sprinkled a lil' Coke in my weed to take the edge off as I waited until Cache came back home.

***

Cache

The morning came faster than I thought it would. Well, that's what I assumed when I looked out the mesh ironed window. The sky was still dark, I didn't give a damn, because I was looking forward to my free collect phone call.

"Cache P! Bitch, that's you?" I looked over and it was my girl K.O. I knew she got knocked but I didn't think she was still in jail.

"Girl, yeah," I answered jumping off the top bunk, rubbing my crusty face so I could get a clear view before I hugged her. I was so glad to see someone I knew.

"Damn bitch, you still locked up?" I asked knowing damn well it couldn't be me.

"Bitch, fuck no. Girl, you know how I do. I jump bail every time they set it. I just came back yesterday. We both should get a bail set this morning so get ready because they will call us in a minute. What you in for, though? I know this ain't even yo' type of hype," she said.

"Bitch I finally got that hoe, Angel—"

"Cache Price, lockdown!" the C.O. yelled before I could tell K.O. what happened.

"Bitch, what you did?" K.O. asked me.

"Fuck if I know. You know I'm new to this shit, not true like you." I walked off to see what the fuck C.O. was talking 'bout.

"Your urine test came back positive for Cocaine. It's just procedure to lock you down for the safety of the population."

The Fuck? I looked with my face twisted up. "I don't do drugs!"

"That's what they all say, now, let's go."

Could this shit get any worse? One def had some explaining to do!

"Cache Price," my name was finally called. This was my first time going through this, but I assumed to do what everyone else did. I walked up to the podium stating my name, date of birth, and address.

"Your bail is set at seventy-five thousand for Aggravated Assault. Are you going to be able to make bail? If not, you can sit and wait on sentencing."

Sentencing? "Actually, your honor I been trying to—"

"Yes, she will be able to post bail," I heard a voice at the back of the courtroom. I knew it was One without even looking back. I have never been so happy and hateful to see that bitch in my life. If I was mad with her, it all went out the window at that moment.

An hour later, I was processed out and back on the street in no time. After signing papers with the bailsman, he made sure to tell me that I could be facing serious time. The Perez family wasn't letting this go. He told me that Angel had undergone surgery and survived it but would never look the same. Apparently, I worked her over pretty good. I didn't want to think about that shit no more than I had to. I needed some weed bad.

Knasir has been at his grandparents' house for like a week. I missed my lil' man. Being locked up made me realize what I put on the line. I was going to see my baby today. Plus, I didn't want to deal with One's ass. I did plan on confronting her ass, though. When I walked outside the parish jail, she and Reign were waiting on me. I took in One's appearance and she did not look like her usually self. Her eyes were bloodshot, and she looked as if she not gotten any sleep.

Even though I was mad, I hugged both my friends. I did miss them but that's what being locked up did to you.

"Cache, I'm sorry—" One said but before she could finish, I told her save that shit.

"It's not the time or place for this," I laid the law, walking off to sit in the passenger seat. I wanted the hoe to know she was def in the doghouse.

Later that day, Reign was dropped off and I was back at home in my comfort zone. I was still angry with One. I'd been chilling in my own zone listening to my iPod while on my IG account.

"So, you going to continue to igg me like I don't exist?" One asking jerking my earplugs out my ear.

"Really?" I asked her, cocking my head to the side.

"Yeah, really! Fucking right. What you mean? The shit not cool. You act like I wanted that shit to pop off! The fuck you want from me?"

She had better get the fuck out my face is the look that I gave her. "This is what I want from you, One. I need you to tell me how the fuck did I end up in jail because of a jealous ass bitch you couldn't keep ya mouth off. How the fuck did we make it to where we are? And why in the fuck did I have Coke show up on my drug test, huh? You know what fuck all the rest of that shit. Explain the Coke to me, baby, because, right now, I'm not too much fucking feeling yo' ass!"

She looked at me like a deer caught in headlights. Finally, she found the words she spoke. "You must've picked up one of my blunts I had around the house." She hung her head.

"So, you still fucking with that shit! I thought we were above that shit?" Not understanding what the fuck she was saying. That explains why I felt the way I did every time I smoked weed with her. As for me picking the shit up on my own was a lie. She had to be slipping it on me.

"I can't help it, the shit takes the edge off."

"That's not a fucking excuse. Whenever you can come up with something better than that holla at me, I'm out," I said grabbing my car keys.

"Where you are you going?" she asked, coming behind me.

"I'll call you when I get there. Right now, I can't stand to look at yo' fucking face."

When I got in my car, she didn't try to stop me. She knew she had fucked up and so did I because even though this hoe had me hated by people, I couldn't leave. I loved her. Even though my mind said go, my heart pulled me towards her. I don't know when it happened or how, but our friendship had become dangerous. We had crossed a line that should have never been crossed. Before I made any decision, I just needed to get away.

CHAPTER 18

CACHE

An hour later, I was joined with my baby. Nothing else in the world at the moment mattered. I received a sense of peace being around him.

"He reminds me so much of his father," Mrs. Duncan said when she entered the room

"He does," I agreed while continuing to play with him.

"When will he be coming back to stay with you? I'm not trying to rush you—to be honest, I'm just concerned about you," she said.

"Don't be, I'm good. I have just been trying to get my life back on track," I told her not wanting to tell her about my arrest last night.

"Okay, well I hope you can stay until dinner gets ready. You can use some meat on them bones."

"I can't, I have to go to work tonight but maybe next time."

Mrs. Duncan always made me feel like she had me under her microscope. I understood it was her just wanting the best for me. I felt smothered, I didn't need her to know I still didn't have a job and was on the verge of being on the streets and on my ass if I didn't get it together.

"I understand, I'm glad you've stopped by. It was good seeing you. We miss you around here. We will keep Knasir as long as you need us to. I know it might seem that I don't understand the way you feel but I do. Just as well as you have lost a husband, I've lost a son. We're feeling the same pain, just from two different perspectives, baby. So yes, I understand. One bit of advice I will give you is don't let life bring you down. This life we live we go through things. We will see things and even though it hurts, life is something we should grow stronger from. On your face, I see years that have passed you by and I mean the struggle. Just because you look around me and see this glamorous life, it doesn't mean it didn't take blood, sweat, and so many tears. But what I will tell you is God is what brought us through, and he is the glue that kept us together throughout the years. He will also keep you if you let him, but you have to allow him to do so." Mrs. Duncan walked off after speaking her peace.

Something inside told me no matter how I tried to hide my wrongdoing to her, I always felt transparent. Instead of going home, because I still wasn't ready to deal with One. I ended up at a hotel after leaving my in-laws house. I felt guilt-ridden and wanted to escape everything, including myself. I stopped by a corner store called S.P.I and grabbed me a bottle of liquor. Once I left the store, I went over to where the two young dudes were selling CDs, flicks, and Muslim oils.

"What's good, fine lady? How can we help you?" the shorter, stocky one asked.

"I'm just looking, right now," I said continuing to look around.

These CDs had to be going for a dollar because everything today is all about technology. I don't even think cars are being made with CD players anymore but if they like it, I love it. The hustle never stops.

"Damn, what's up with you, ma?"

I know dude was talking to me, but I kept it pushing because I had other shit on my mind. Plus, I hadn't entertained anyone since—that doesn't include One.

"A'ight, I see how you acting. You think you all that and don't fuck with real niggas." That nigga had straight hit a nerve.

"First the fuck off, let me tell you something! I do think I'm all that for several reasons. One, I take care of me. Two, I got my own whip. And three, I pay my own bills. As for what you see, it's what you get. Appearance don't make me, I make me! So, before you come fucking with me about real niggas, real niggas don't judge a book by its cover." I turned back around and continued what I was doing, minding my own damn business.

"Damn, ma, let me apologize for coming at you sideways. I didn't know you were having a bad day. My name's Tony and you?"

So, even though I didn't want to be bothered, I couldn't deny dude was dripping in ice. That Jesus piece was sweet! He was dark-skinned with a mouth full of golds and dreads taller than me. No lie, dude was hot, and I bet he was the one driving the all-black ultrasleek 2019 Maybach. I dropped the bad girl attitude, right then and there I made up my mind, I had plans for this nigga.

"Cache Price," I responded extending my hand, looking forward to something new.

"Word?" He looked at me smiling

"Yeah, it's like that." I smiled back.

"I like that. So, can we exchange numbers, IGs?"

"We can do that." I pulled my phone out taking his number and giving him mine.

"When can I hit you?"

"Mmmm, whenever you free I guess."

"A'ight, cool. Ma check this out, how bout I take you out tonight? Just you and me."

"I don't know, I'm kinda tired. So, how 'bout I call you before I leave town?"

"Tomorrow isn't promised, let's live for now. Besides, I would hate to have to spend my birthday all by myself when I can have someone like you on my arm. When dude smiled, I couldn't let my no be a no. He had def' changed my mind to yes. Nigga got my vote.

"A'ight, cool. Give me time to go shopping and freshen up."

"Take this love. No way I'ma let you come to my city and not treat you like a queen." He went inside his pocket and came out with a knot.

After he gave me the money, we went our separate ways with promises to link up later. The first thing I did after leaving was head to the Mall of Louisiana. If I'm going to step out, I planned to give everybody with a set of eyes the business. There is no way I'm going to let these country bum hoes shit on me tonight. I don't know what Tony had planned but whatever it is, I will look my best. I was 'bout to paint the town red. Tonight, I was going hard because I definitely wasn't going home.

CHAPTER 19

ONE

The fuck? Was this hoe really playing on my top? She must didn't know I would catch a hat charge! When C left the house upset, I went right behind her. I was afraid that she would hurt herself, so I followed her. I stayed a few cars back because I didn't need her to know I was staked out. People did stupid shit when upset. Fuck! What else was I supposed to do? She gave me no other choice when she wouldn't tell me where she was headed. Now that I see this bitch was just fine and smiling all in dude's face. This made me not be able to trust her as far as I could throw her. She wasn't even gay, just for me, I think. She couldn't stop smiling in the nigga's face.

I decided to text her once she got in the car after the nigga hit her with a rubber band. Did she know dude or something?

//: Bae, where are you? I texted.

It didn't take her long to respond.

//: Just came from seeing my son.

//: When are you coming home? I hit her back.

//: DK, I think I found a lick.

That made me feel good, I smiled. She was talking 'bout dude from the store.

//: Oh, yeah. So, you back in the game?

//: Maybe, the nigga looked loaded. He wants to take me out tonight.

Now I started to get mad, but I thought about it for a second. She really didn't have to keep it real. She didn't know that I had been watching her from afar. I took her word for what it was and texted back.

//: Go for it.

//: Cool, on my way to the mall, his treat. I'll lookout.

I headed back the opposite way. I had nothing to worry 'bout. She didn't lie so everything was cool with me.

//: Love you! She texted that shit made me feel good.

//: Love you too.

Cache

Day turned into night and I was doing some last-minute touches. I was fully dressed, so the only thing left was to apply my MAC nude gloss and a splash of Chanel No.5 would do the trick. I took a look in the mirror and loved what I saw. I blew a kiss at myself, took another shot of my drink and headed out the door to my rose gold 745.

I finally made it to Club Vibes and immediately knew I was not about to stand in this long ass line in my Jimmy Choos. I pulled my cell out and dial Tony's number.

"What up, ma? I hope you ain't changing yo' mind?" he asked over the loud club music.

"No, actually I didn't. I'm outside."

"A'ight, I'm 'bout to meet you. Park in the VIP section. I'm on my way out."

By the time I made my way to a parking space, Tony was waiting on me. He was looking like money. I noticed something about him that I didn't notice before. Even though I could tell he had money, I didn't see the swag the he possessed. Damn! He cleaned up nice. When I stepped out of my whip, I not only commanded his attention, but everyone around admired me as well.

"You really look good tonight, ma." He kissed me on my cheek and extended his hand out and taking mine.

"Thank you. I know you didn't expect me to come any other way." I smiled and walked off sassily as he held the door open and I stepped inside the club.

In the streets of B.R. this the only way we living.
The good die young and all the others go to prison.
The streets ain't safe and I ain't looking for religion.
In the streets or B.R.—

Gates was on the stage performing when we entered. Baton Rouge was live tonight and if I knew I would be out here partying, I would have definitely told Reign to take this trip with me. Matter of fact, I think I'll send her a text.

//: Club Vibes. Come thru. $$$

I knew after sending that text she was already on the way. I'll give her an hour and she would be walking through the door. I was straight putting these hoes to shame tonight. Killing 'em. D.O.A. I must admit, there were some fly bitches in here, but I was still holding the number one spot down. When Reign came through like a storm, it'll be double the trouble.

"Mane, who shawty is T? Bitch fire as a muthafucka."

"I doubt she fucks muthas so watch ya mouth, Slim. This one mine," Tony said with no emotion. Deadly.

"She should've been fucking somebody's mutha cuz I swear on God I would love to see that shit." Everybody started laughing. Not with him but at him. The nigga was too wasted.

"You right, my nigga. It'll be me joining them not yo' bum ass. Everybody, this my girl, Cache. From here on out respect her."

Right then and there I knew Tony would become my sponsor. The nigga came through like a wave demanding respect and whether they wanted to or not they gave it. That made me know he was that nigga. Tonight, for some reason I felt like a brand new me. I wasn't sure why. Maybe it was because I felt free, but it could've been the shots I kept taking to the head. Or maybe it was because Cache ruled everything around me once again.

CHAPTER 20

CACHE

It's been three months since I've been seeing Tony and I had done everything but moved my shit from my crib to his. Tony forbid that I leave his side. He said it's because he wanted to keep his girl protected but I know he started acting overprotective ever since I put Miss Kitty on that ass. Between trying to keep him and One on chill, I been running like the Energizer Bunny. One had become so possessive as if I was a pair of Jimmy Choo heels. The shit was bugging the fuck out of me. Shit between us had gotten old and I just wasn't with it no more.

Now don't get me wrong, I love her but loved it even more when she sucked my pussy. I haven't found anyone yet that could take that number one spot. I guess that's why I couldn't let her go. I loved having my cake and eating it too. She been on my ass though like white on rice. She kept questioning me about when I was gon' set the shit up to hit Tony's safe.

The thing is I had fucked around and started falling for the nigga. His testosterone was just something I also wasn't trying to give up either. To buy me some time, I kept telling her the nigga hasn't given me the code yet and I also kept feeding her pussy on the platter to keep her on hold.

I pulled into the projects, and as usual, Reign had her sexy gangster ass outside thuggin' with the fellas.

"Damn bitch, I see you always outside thuggin' with the fellas," I said what I thought.

"I see dude got you in something nice, huh?" she said hugging me

"Yeah, you know I never put it down for the minimum."

"Why should you? Every bitch not blessed with good pussy."

"Heyyy!" We both screamed at the same time slapping hands.

"So, what is it that you have planned for us?" she asked.

"Girl, nothing. I just wanted to drop by before I go check in with this hoe, One," I said while she shook her head.

"Bitch! I don't know how you do it. Her ass has got so crazy. You need to cut that hoe off before it's too late. You already know the hoe been lacing the weed with fucking Coke. That hoe was all the way down bad. She knew that shit ain't you no more and for her to carry the shit like that? Come on, C, no apology in this world is big enough to forgive that shit." She shook her head.

"Bitch, I know but you know how it is when a nigga has you weak at the knees. She got a bitch still trembling and I haven't fucked her since last week," I said thinking about how I couldn't wait till later.

"Mane I hear that shit, but you already know I ain't never been a big fan of the hoe. Only on the strength of you."

"I feel ya."

"You better feel me a lil' more than that. Look at that nigga Zane and Mascot. I know them niggas regret fucking over her now."

"Them niggas deserved that shit, though. No ifs, ands, or buts. The crazy hoe gon' think you deserve it, too, C. How long you think she gon' go for that bullshit 'bout not having the nigga code? This, not the DaVinci code, baby."

I couldn't lie she was really spitting some real shit. I just didn't know how I would be able to keep my shit in pocket. Something had to give before something gave in.

***

One

I couldn't stop pacing the floor waiting on Cache's ass. I had really started getting impatient with this shit she was trying to pull. *"Just give me time."* I was tired of hearing that shit. She made me feel like she was really fucking with dude or something. My word is my word, so I'ma give her ass a few more weeks. If she hasn't made any moves by then, I'ma do what I have to do and dig enough dirt to bury her ass. But as I said, for now, I'ma give it time.

I placed some gloves on my hand before I went to the safe, I had moved to Cache's house. Whenever I felt overly emotional, I pulled my baby out to clean it. If I didn't trust in a soul, my gun was authentic. My trigger finger never let me down yet. Ever since I was a little girl, I had been infatuated with artillery. Thanks to Commander Watkins, my father. He had been a part of the military compound in Guadalajara where he met the princess of that city in Mexico. Emilia Hidalgo, daughter of drug lord, Emiliano.

I didn't have to live the life I was living but I did. I could be with my family in Guadalajara but I hated Emiliano. He had my father and mother killed because they wanted out of the life. My grandfather wasn't having that shit, he felt it was my mother's birthright to be a part of the Cartel. My grandfather believed that my mother betrayed his trust all because she fell in love and wanted to give me a better life. Falling in love was her downfall but I couldn't blame her for the shit. Fuck look at me, I was ready to lay the world down at Cache feet is asked.

After putting every part of my firearm back together, I heard a knock at the door. I knew it was Cache. I placed the gun on the table and went and took the chain off the door.

"Hey, baby," she said stepping inside kissing me like she missed me.

"What's up with you?" I asked.

"Nothing, just glad I could away from that nigga."

"Oh, yeah. Sounds like you ready to go through with hitting 'em?"

"I wish baby, but not yet."

"Why not?" I asked watching her facial expression very close.

"The nigga ain't give me the code yet. I told you just give me a few weeks." She walked to where I was cleaning my gun.

I walked behind her, wrapping my arms around her waist. "Well, I need you home. Me and Knasir." I gave her my puppy dog eyes that always made her melt.

"What are you doing with this just hanging out?" she asked picking up my first bitch.

"You know when my nerves get bad, I love having my bitch close. Especially, when I don't have my bitch close," I said slapping her on the ass. “Let me get that, I’ma go put it back in the safe. I know how you feel about them.”

“A’ight, I’ma go get in the tub and get in some more comfortable clothes.”

“Cool, take your time.”

When she went to the bathroom, I started toward her purse. I went through her phone to see if there was anything she was hiding from me. I went through her pictures to see what she and this nigga had been up to. A picture spoke a thousand words so when I opened her gallery, I saw selfies of the two. The next picture fucked me up though because it was a picture of Knasir and her sister, A’nett with a caption that said, *World’s greatest BIG SIS.* What does that mean? Was A’nett her daughter and not really her sister? I didn’t understand. I guess that explains why she has always been so constant with dropping money off in her grandmother’s mailbox. Every family always has a secret and I guess this is something her Bible-toting, over religious grandmother, wanted to be kept under wraps.

As I continued to go through her phone, I ran across a recording that had been recorded over a year and a half ago. I wondered what could have been that important for her to have kept this long. I hit play so that I could hear what the hell it was.

“Cache, would you marry me?”

“Yes, yes, yes!”

“My nigga she said—" Then there were gunshots.

Damn, she held on to this.

“What are you doing?”

“What?”

I was caught.

“Don’t fucking what me! What are you doing?”

“Nothing, I thought I heard your phone ring.”

“Give me my shit. Why can’t you just trust me? This the shit I be talking ‘bout.”

“Fuck you mean the shit you be talking ‘bout? You talking about me to that nigga? So, what you plan on leaving me, huh?”

“Don’t start that stupid ass nonsense,” she said walking off.

I couldn't help myself, I went behind her and grabbed her ponytail. "What, I don't fuck you good enough no more? The nigga fucks you better?" I asked kissing on her neck.

"Mmmm, no," she moaned.

"No what? I don't fuck you right? What is it?"

"Yessss, you the only one that can fuck me exactly how I need."

"So, why in the fuck you still with that bitch ass nigga? What, I'ma have to kill him or what?" I asked slipping my manicured hand in her pants. "Is that what I'ma have to do, huh?"

"Nooo," she said breathless.

"Why? Convince me."

"This pussy for you, bae. Ooweee."

"You sure?" I asked ready to fuck the shit outta her. My pussy was so wet.

"Yessss."

I still wasn't convinced, though. In the back of my mind, I still felt her ass was playing tug-a-war between me and this bitch nigga, Tony. Maybe I was more like the drug lord than I thought because I was ready to kill everyone she loved so that her heart would only love me.

CHAPTER 21

CACHE

The next morning, I woke up feeling like a stranger in my own home. This bitch was really crazy. I couldn't believe that she really thought I would be a part of another one of her assassinations. The very first time that shit happened with Thadius a few years back, it wasn't supposed to happen. For a while, the shit had me fucked up, but I quickly shook back. How I saw it, better him than me.

After washing my face and brushing my teeth, I grabbed my phone. "Damn." I had a lot of missed calls and even a few text messages. Somebody really was trying to get in touch with me. All calls were from my family. Lord, please don't let nothing be wrong with A'nett. I called Mo-Mo CW and on the first ring she picked up.

"My baby!"

"Grams, what's going on? What's so urgent?"

"It's ya momma. Come quickly, she don't have much longer to live," she said through tears.

I knew something serious had happened. I never knew my grandmother to be so fragile, not even when she lost two sons not long apart from each other.

"I'm on the way. Where are y'all?" I asked while tears started flowing freely.

"Baton Rouge General Mid City."

After I hung up the phone, I woke One up letting her know what was going on. I wasn't in my right mind to drive by myself, so she came with me. She didn't ask any questions and I was so grateful for that. I didn't know anything myself. It didn't take us long to arrive. When I entered the hospital's waiting room, everything from there moved in slow motion. All my family was hugged up, comforting each other and crying.

I already knew what the verdict was when I caught my grandmother's eye. She walked up to me, grabbed me in her arms and before I could fall into her arms, shedding my own tears, my bro and sis Carnell, Chanel, and my big baby A'nett came hugged me.

Right then and there, I knew I had to make this shit right. A'nett needed to know that I was her mother and the woman that had just died was *my* mother. I didn't want to carry this shit on my chest anymore.

This was a family secret that no one talked about. I was eleven years old when my virginity was snatched from me in order to pay off one of my mother's drug debts. Consequently, I became pregnant. My mother, her mother, and myself were the only three people in this world who knew the sordid details.

I wanted to tell A'nett everything but what good would it do right now? I asked myself. If it ain't broke don't fix it, Momo CW always said. And today had been tough enough, without adding to it, so I decided to keep the secret a little longer, while I tried to find a way to cope with my loss.

After leaving the hospital, I had to get away. I needed my own space. When me and One made it back home, I didn't give an explanation. I just left. My grams had explained that my mother had been living with H.I.V. for over 15 years. What I didn't understand was how, and how in the hell I didn't know? When was anyone going to tell me? I mean, I am her oldest child. It just wasn't right. Then on top of all that crazy, as it may sound, that wasn't actually what killed her. Colon and Lung Cancer is what did it.

Within a few days, the cancer spread, leaving her blind. My grams told me Ann said she didn't want to live like that. She didn't come in this world that way and she wasn't going to remain here that way. I just couldn't get that shit. What did she mean? Did she forget she had people that loved her and would miss her? I kept asking myself how she could just up and leave without even saying goodbye.

I drove to S.P. I. to get a bottle of gin. I got back in my car, driving straight to Tony's house. I needed to see him. By the time I made it, I was fucked up. I didn't give a fuck though. This was just as bad as losing Knowledge.

"What's wrong, Cache?" he asked as soon as he saw me.

I couldn't even open my mouth to tell him. For the second time that day, I fell into someone's arms and just cried. For the next few days, everything was a blur. I didn't even make the funeral arrangements with my family, I couldn't. Once again, I had lost someone close to my heart that I could never see or talk to again and it hurt. I had no understanding. If I could have been there more would things have been different? I guess that's something I'll never know.

"Are you ready?" Tony asked.

"Yeah," was what my mouth said but I really wasn't ready to put my mom to rest.

I knew it had to be done so I had no choice but to get up. I wouldn't miss this for the world. Ann would want me to celebrate her life, but it was hard. I tried finding her strength in me but I'll never be as strong as she was. I couldn't even touch half of what she possessed. When we finally made it to Hall Davis and Son Funeral Home on Scenic Highway there were cars lining the street with family and friends. There were even people there to see if she was really gone.

People I had no clue even knew my mother. It really touched my heart to see two of my mother's oldest friends. Al and the other person, a lady that I couldn't remember her name, but I know she loved my mom like a sister. She was clean, she no longer was an addict and when she did get clean, she came back for Ann. Ann being Ann though was stubborn. She once told me she was a soldier and took the bull by its horn. Once the service started, I was physically here but I wasn't mentally.

I somehow found the strength to put everything together, including the obituary, which announced:

Homegoing Celebration for
Sandra Ann Tenner Price

-Sunrise- December 19, 1967-Sunset- November 25, 2018

Friday, Dec. 7, 2018

11:00 Am

Hall Davis and Son

Sandra Ann Tenner Moore 50, went to glory on November 25, 2018, in the comfort of her long-time residence. Sandra was the widow of her late husband Larry Carnell Price Sr. They shared many years of marriage and are now joined again in heaven.

Born in Natchez, MS. She was the daughter of Cora J. Warner and Johnny Tenner Sr. She was a long-time user at Jordan Stone, in Ethel, La. Pastored by Revered Richardson. She will be remembered for her one of kind personality and being the light of the room—Rest in Peace, Momma.

A host of family members got up to speak on how my mother was a good person, how she loved to cook and listen to music. As for me, I felt like a prisoner, shackled with chains and cuffs. As bad as I wanted to get up and speak for my mother, I couldn't. She knew the words I had for her were written on both of our hearts and they were only shared between the two of us.

Sandra Ann Tenner Moore 50, went to glory on November 25, 2018, in the comfort of her long-time residence. Sandra was the widow of her late husband Larry Carnell Price Sr. They shared many years of marriage and are now joined again in heaven.

Born in Natchez, MS. She was the daughter of Cora J. Warner and Johnny Tenner Sr. She was a long-time user at Jordan Stone, in Ethel, La. Pastored by Revered Richardson. She will be remembered for her one of kind personality and being the light of the room—Rest in Peace, Momma.

CHAPTER 22

CACHE

3 Months Later

I wondered if my Ann was disappointed in me. It had been 3 months since she'd been gone and shit just hadn't been the same. I started back fucking with that Coke again, but this time it wasn't because of One. I hadn't heard from her since I left the house that day. I just couldn't face her, especially now that I just left her hanging. Me and Tony were still together and once again, I found myself pregnant. I wasn't ready to do this shit all over again either and that's exactly why I didn't have the balls to tell Tony how I truly felt. This being his first child, he was expecting me to have this baby. Fuck, I don't even have the ones that are already here. So, what made this nigga think I wanted this one? Don't get me wrong, I love my kids and I've been making arrangements so that the two of them could come stay with us.

Time seemed to be flying. It just felt as if it was yesterday, I lost the love of my life. Now, look at me, trying to fill the hole in my heart. I started going against everything I ever stood for when I fell back into the belly of the beast. But who am I to intervene? Don't people say everything is written and was supposed to happen exactly as they are? I needed God, but of course, he wasn't anywhere to be found. I continued to self-medicate and sex my pain away.

"Hey, bae, what you doing so long in the bathroom? You good in there?"

"Yeah, I'm okay. I'll be out in a minute!" I yelled back through the doors. I needed a taste of nose candy and as I've said, he had no clue. Two minutes later, I had cleaned up and was walking out with a twinkle in my eyes.

"Come here, give me a kiss," Tony said kissing me. "Is it morning sickness again?" he asked because I have been telling him that's my reason for always being in the bathroom

"Yeah, but I'm feeling way better now, and I actually have something better than a kiss." I smiled.

At least that's what I thought, pushing him on the bed. I got on all fours crawling toward him like a feline, purring and all. He already knew what time it was and started unzipping his pants.

"We got to make this quick, Phat," he said eagerly, knowing he was in for a treat. I agreed because I also had things to do but first, I needed to get him off.

"You know once I put that neck on you, it doesn't take long at all. Nigga lay back and shut up." Of course, I was going to do my best when it came to him. Tony always treated me well, throwing money every time I popped him off. I got so used to playing housewife that finding a job and my hustle went out the window.

"I got to make a run, plus me and my niggas going out."

"I thought we were going out," I said pretending like him going out with his boys had nothing to do with me.

Before he could answer, I took his dick and stuffed it into my mouth. He was def' 'bout to get the best head ever. Trina ain't have shit on me. Fuck a bad bitch, I am that bitch! I straight deep throated him. After hitting him off like I was a contestant in the Amazing Race, I jetted out the door like a hooker without her pimp's money. I didn't even have time to spit. I swallowed and took the tip of my manicured nail and wiping the cracks of mouths.

"Hello?" I answered the phone on the first ring.

"Bitch, where you at?" Reign asked.

"Damn, hoe. Give me a lil' minute, I'ma be on my way. Don't be tripping and shit."

"How far are you?"

"I'ma be pulling up in a minute, hoe."

Before she could say anything smart, I hung up. I don't need Reign's ass blowing my high. I dialed one of Tony's boys next, who didn't hesitate to answer.

"What's good, lil momma?"

"I'm tryna see what you got for me."

"Whatever you want but you gon' have to come with it this time." He laughed

"Nigga, I got money. I always come with it. Don't stunt on me," I said ready to spend.

"No ma, ya cash not good here no more."

"So, it's like that?"

"Yeah, it's like that. Fair exchange ain't no robbery," he said seriously.

I was only hesitant for a moment. I was running out of time, so I was like just get this shit over with. "A'ight, I'm on my way. Give me five minutes."

When I finally pulled up to his trap house, I was fully in disguise. Throwing on my blonde hooker wig and Dolce shades as I stepped out of my ride. I didn't need anyone noticing me. By right, I had no business over here. If Tony found this shit out, I could go ahead and consider myself as good as dead.

The thing is, my drug habit was progressing by the day and I was too ashamed to reach out for help. I feared that I would be judged, so to cope I just continued to tell myself that everything was okay. I headed around to the back door and did this knock that was required for me to gain access.

He opened the door with this big ass Kool-Aid smile. "I'm glad you could come through, lil momma," he said, stepping to the side so that I could step inside.

"Glad I could come? Negro, please! Let's get this shit over with." I walked past him. Like he said, fair exchange ain't a robbery. I had what he wanted, and he had what I needed. I kept that thought to myself, though, holding my handout for issue. No sense in pretending. He handed me an eight ball of powder and I headed straight to the bathroom.

On my way, I took notice for the first time that Marciano's trap looked more like someone's home, instead of the average trap. I just took it as him hustling smart. The cops would least expect this house had traffic coming through like a Wendy's drive-thru at lunch hour. When I entered the beautifully equipped bathroom, I took a seat at the vanity and placed my Coke on the table so I could do my thing. This was one reason I liked fucking with Marc. He had everything

I needed right here. He always broke a bitch off, plus he didn't judge me.

As soon as I snorted a line, I heard the bathroom door open. I knew Marc was coming to stake his claim, Grim Reaper style. He enjoyed foreplay and I did, too. Well, under the circumstances, Marc knew to get me high first and all was fair game. I hated to admit it, but I loved getting fucked when I was high, but I also didn't mind doing the fucking either. Everything was good between the two of us, and as long as the nigga kept my secret, I kept his.

"Get out yo' clothes," he demanded.

I obeyed, when I was completely naked, I laid back on the floor, spreading my legs. As soon as I did, the cool air flowing in from the open door attacked my already hardened clit. I couldn't help myself. It felt like I was having an out of body experience. I don't know where he gets his Coke from but so it was the best. Some way, somehow without even thinking twice, my hand found my clit and started doing its own thing. It had a mind of its own. My pussy was already wet. Within a few seconds, I came so hard, but I was greedy. That wasn't enough and I wanted more.

Marc just stood there looking at my fat juicy pussy while stroking back and forth, back and forth. I could feel myself about to cum, so I sped up.

"Stop," he commanded just when I was at my peak.

He came down to the floor with me, laid back, dick at full attention. I pulled out a bag from under the sink, took out the things I needed, and got into the 69 position. We never actually had sexual intercourse, but always oral sex, along with some of his other things we do.

I popped a mint in my mouth and deep throated him. Not much of a dick sucker but the way he ate pussy, I wasn't complaining. The nigga made you suck it happily in return. His head game was that vicious. My head game isn't what made the nigga's toes curl. After he was strong as steel, I grabbed what I went in the bag for, a dildo. Like I said, there was no physical penetration from him to me. I turned the vibrator on and inserted it into his back door.

"Fucking right, fuck that shit," he moaned in excitement.

"Nigga shut the fuck up and eat the pussy," it was my turn to make demands. "Nigga make me cum—fuck!" I had to admit, the shit turned me on or maybe because I knew at the end, I'd be rewarded handsomely.

After our fuck fest, which lasted longer than I expected, I hopped in his shower, changed into my party outfit and was ready to go. He popped me off with 2 stacks and another ball of Coke. On my way out, Marc grabbed me by the arm.

"What's up?" I asked ready to go because just that fast, I was over him.

I was already late. That's when he kissed me. I kissed him back, but not as affectionate as he would have liked. I had to keep the nigga in my back pocket.

"I'll see you tonight," he said.

When I pulled apart from him. I didn't even respond. I just walked out. Something had to give, I could not keep doing this to myself.

CHAPTER 23

ONE

When it finally hit me that I had been played, I was fucking furious. Cache was a dead bitch! So, I hoped she was enjoying the rest of her time with that nigga. I knew the hoe thought shit was all peaches and cream, but I was too righteous to this hoe to just lay down at the cross. I wasn't ready to confess to my sins and move on. Oh no, I planned to get even, and I knew exactly how to hit her where it hurts.

I'd just been ducked off waiting on the right time to strike. I'd been following her, stupid bitch! I wondered if the nigga Tony knew this bitch was fucking his boy. I made sure to take a picture of her coming out of his house. I wanted to fuck with her head. I laughed as I pulled off without her noticing me.

She was having a surprise party for the nigga and I was invited! Well not by her but I'm inviting my fucking self, straight-party crashing. I had a rude awakening for her ass. First things first though, I needed to get ready for the party. I had the perfect outfit. My make-up would be perfect and so is my plan.

The party would be at Club Lounge. That wasn't my part of town and I didn't know anybody over there but as always, money talked and bullshit walked. These days muthafuckas would drop a dime on they own momma just to have two nickels to rub together.

After getting dressed and ready for the night, I looked in the mirror and knew my plan would go perfect. I grabbed my purse, which held my gun inside and proceeded out the door. I know muthafuckas wondered why I still stayed at Cache's place when I had my own shit. For one, I held on to the hope that one day her trifling life ass would bring that sweet pussy back to me, but boy was I wrong. I don't know what this nigga put on her but I'm going to find out tonight.

When I made it to the Club Lounge, it was ten o'clock. It had not gotten packed yet but soon I knew people were going to start rolling in. Instead of waiting in the line, I walked to the front like I do every time I go anywhere. Without talking, I placed two

Franklins in the bouncer's hand kissing him on both cheeks as if we knew each other. Discreetly, he looked at what I placed in his hand and opened the rope to let me through. Just like that, I was in.

CHAPTER 24

CACHE

Later that night, the club was packed, but Tony's ass still hadn't made it.

"Bitch, where this nigga at?" Dream asked.

I could tell that they were getting impatient.

"Girl, I don't know. Let me call to see where they at." But when I looked at my phone, I had a picture of me coming out of Marc's house. WTF? Who the fuck was playing games?

"Do you! Work the floor or something. They got so much money in this bitch. Tony's not the only man with the plan. I told you hoes to show these niggas how we do it! Turn this bitch up! One man don't stop the show."

As I started walking off, Tony started calling me. I tried to exit the club before I answered, but it was too late. When I stepped into the cool air, I pressed redial. Just when I did, I could hear music in the distance. I looked to the East and saw an assembly line of tricked out old schools.

I hurried back inside knowing that it was Tony and his boys. The only one who knew I would be here tonight was Marc. I got him to set the shit up and kept the shit a secret right along with all the other stuff we share. By the time I made it back inside, my girls had got it jumping and I promise, they didn't disappoint. I hurried to the dressing room to change and power up. My mind went right back to the pic. Who knew?

"Reign, let that hoe Dream know to wrap that shit up on stage. The real show is about to start in forty-five." I had a surprise for Tony, something I knew he would enjoy. When I finished dressing in my come fuck me outfit, I texted Marc to see if they had made it inside.

//: Yes. He texted back.

//: Send him to the private room.

In the private room, I had it set up with all types of shit that I knew he would like. I even had fruit to feed him.

"Bitch, you ready?" I asked Dream when she came into the dressing room.

"Shit, yeah. Born," she said, smacking my ass. "I've been waiting for this moment."

We both threw back X pills. Ten minutes later, we were rolling to the max on blue dolphins. What I didn't know is if Dream was speaking on been ready for me or my nigga. That hoe wouldn't want to cross that line though because her ass would be pushing flowers by the end of the week. I felt like I was on cloud 9 without the clouds like I had an *S* on my chest. We finally made it to the private room. Dream was on my heels.

When I stepped inside, I got the surprise of my life. Tony was sitting on the couch with his head thrown back, enjoying some random bitch between his legs. My mind screamed to run up and beat both their fuckin asses, but the way this bitch was doing her shit—One! *The fuck?* Was what my mind screamed. I knew from the tramp stamp on her back. *Cache Ruled Everything Around Me!* Just when I thought I was rid of this hoe, she snuck up on me just like the snake I always known her to be.

Tony's head popped up and his eyes flew wide open, so did One's. She wasn't at all surprised. Her face held a smirk because she knew she had me cornered. That's when I put it together, she was the one who sent the picture, which was her way of daring me to pop off. My heart was racing fast from the X pills, I could hardly breathe. Tony started putting his clothes on once he pushed One off his dick. The nigga wanted to plead his case and I just wasn't up for it. I had to get the fuck away from them. He didn't even know this hoe was out to hurt me.

"Nah, stay there!" I screamed.

"It's not what you think," Tony started explaining.

By this time, One was off the floor and on the sectional with her legs crossed eating my fruits.

"Nigga, shut up!" I pushed him back on the couch without him saying a word.

This hoe wanted to play this game. I was about to give her what she wanted. Since his dick was still rock hard, I pulled it back out.

I straddled his lap while pushing my thong to the side, easing my love box down on his stick until he filled me up. I started grinding my hips and pushing down so that the tip of his dick hit my g-spot every time. One must have known my clit started throbbing. She latched on sucking and flicking her tongue like she invented giving head. Either that or the X pill was working me overtime.

I placed both of my open palms on his thighs, I lifted myself up slightly. Up down. Up down. The last time I went up and down, I felt a finger slip into my back door. From my pussy to my stomach to my tits, she kissed. I pulled her face to mine kissing her deeply missing that strawberry MAC she knew I loved so much.

"Fuck." The way that she made my body tingle, I forgot all about Tony.

Other than me grinding on his pole trying to cum, he was here for nothing. As I continued to ride his dick, she used her fingers to flick my clit. The shit drove me insane. Not long after, I came so hard. I got myself together quickly. I stood up and kissed Tony passionately and I did One the same. I knew fucking with him tonight would be my last time.

"Happy Birthday." I walked out of the private room and out of his life. I didn't need any of my demons destroying him like I said, something had to give.

***

Cache

Without even changing or cleaning myself up, I slipped back into my sheer robe and grabbed my shit before Reign, and I bounced.

"Girl, what happened? Why we leaving, you good?"

"Actually, I'm great." I smiled but what I wanted to say was, "It wasn't fun when the rabbit had the gun." Yeah, I cheated on Tony, but I felt my shit was justified. "I'm going back to the city with you but first take me to the nigga's spot."

Without asking why she headed in the direction of his crib. Tonight, I realized the shit I had going on with Tony was overrated.

He didn't love me but saw me as a prized possession. As long as I looked pretty and fucked him well, he kept me laced with all the latest shit, but I wanted more than that. How would I achieve it? I wasn't sure but I did have an idea. I remembered my grandmother telling me when I was a little girl that sometimes the only means of transportation is a leap of faith. Back in the day, I didn't understand what she meant but today—well my leap of faith came with what was coming next.

We finally made it to his crib and I immediately went straight to our walk-in closet. He had no clue that I knew his secret. Late at night, whenever he finally decided to come home from doing only God knows what, he went to the closet while pulling out rubber bands of money. The nigga's so dumb that he never looked back to see if I was asleep or not.

"Girl, what the fuck you doing?" Reign asked, standing over my shoulder.

"Leaving his ass. Open this duffle bag," I said tossing her the carry-on, not bothering to look back. One thing I knew for certain about her was when it came down to that bag, she never asked questions. Once I found his stash spot, I was surprised that he didn't have a safe, but only a compartment built in the floor. "Dumb nigga." I shook my head.

"I agree," she said over my shoulder.

Once I took the opening off, being shocked was an understatement. This was his own personal safety box, minus the safety. Money wasn't the only thing he held in here. This shit was straight extortion. Besides the money, there were guns, jewelry, and drugs, lots of it.

"Bitch this the best thing you could have ever done—"

"What the fuck?" I yelled before Reign could finish.

"Girl what?" she asked concerned. I started crying immediately.

"No way, I can't believe this shit."

"This the Cartier watch I brought for Knowledge. Question is, how did this nigga end up with it?"

"Girl, when they started making them bitches, they didn't stop," she said thinking I was tripping.

"Nah, you're right, but they don't come engraved with *My King Forever and Always, K & C.* The K & C stood for Knowledge and Cache.

"So, what you think?" she asked feeling where I was coming from now.

I was afraid to answer the question. If I did, that meant I would have to admit I'd been sleeping with the enemy. I had to do something to make this right! As I continued to pack the bundles of money and drugs, I grabbed a gun also for my protection just in case my plans fell through.

"Let's go," I told Reign.

"Bitch, you gon' leave that? We might as well rob the nigga blind."

"For every action, there is a reaction and when our karma comes around, I don't need a bullet to the head."

I know she didn't understand what I was doing but tomorrow she would. "I need to find a spot to put this," I said, grabbing what I was going to leave.

Then it hit me. I knew exactly where to place it. Once everything was settled, we grabbed everything I came for and headed out the door. Whatever my karma would be will have to wait until later, but for now, I gladly gave Tony his. Well part of it, tomorrow, he would be served.

CHAPTER 25

ONE

I was absolutely proud of myself. I def' was patting myself on the back and o giving myself a standing ovation. But I hope she didn't think that was all I had in store for that ass. If she thought I was finished, she had another thing coming. I was def' on some shit. If I can't have you, no one else can either. Fuck that, I made that hoe. Before me, she wasn't shit and if it wasn't for me, she would have continued to not be shit. I know for a fact she was at the nigga's crib lifting everything out the safe. As I said, we are one and the same. I didn't have to be there either to know. She had no clue, but she was playing into everything I needed her to.

When I saw she and Reign headed out the nigga's crib with two duffels, I know she found the watch I planted. The dumb bitch didn't even have a clue that I killed that nigga Knowledge. That night I was with the nigga Jock. We had been dating for a while. I was trying to move on with my life and put that shit behind me that happened at her party.

The doctors prescribed me all kinds of medicine for my mental instability and for a while it worked. Until that night, when I heard Knowledge ask Cache to marry him, something inside me just clicked. I felt she didn't deserve to be happy unless it was with me. She is what made me happy and brought joy to my life. I knew I didn't need all them fucking pills I was taking. The shit had me moving all robotic.

Without thinking, because wasn't much to think about, I pulled out my baby. I started blasting on both them niggas. They had both died before they could even process what had happened. See, I wasn't really a bad person. At least I didn't let them niggas suffer. Anywho, I was satisfied with my work. This was a job well done. I drove off once they were in the car. I headed in the other direction back to Cache's crib. I knew she wasn't going there. Her ass didn't have the balls to face me.

The next morning when I got up, I got dressed and headed out the door. I was on my way to Mo-Mo C.W.'s house. I had been keeping up with Cache's family more and more. I began to love them and accept them as my own while she was busy running the streets. I continued giving Mo-Mo C.W. money, telling her it was from Cache. Each time she asked why she hadn't stopped by, I would make excuse after excuse by telling them she was still grieving the loss of her mother. Mo-Mo C.W. was always understanding and she would drop it. We would start talking about something else. As we were running it, a school bus stopped in front of the house and A'nett hopped off. She looked so much like Cache she had to be her daughter.

"Hey T.T." A'nett came up to me hugging my neck.

"Hey, baby, how was school?" I asked.

"It was okay, but this ugly boy keeps picking on me." She frowned.

"Sound like you crushing."

"Nope, boys are stupid." Being in middle school I knew was hard for her.

"Yeah, I agree," I told her. "You know what? If it's alright with Mo-Mo C.W. we can go on a shopping spree," I suggested. We both looked her way.

"Well, it's okay with me as long as y'all bring me something nice."

A'nett started jumping up and down excited knowing I would blow a few stacks on her. "We got you Mo-Mo. Let's go T.T." She grabbed my hand and we left.

I grew a motherly love for this child and whatever me and Cache had going on had nothing to do with us.

CHAPTER 26

CACHE

What the fuck this bitch think she was doing with my family? This bitch was insane! Mo-Mo C.W. had to be getting old. No way would she have let me go anywhere with nobody when I was growing up. Not even with family. This bitch was really the devil. I didn't have to worry about her hurting my baby though or my family. I could at least give the bitch that much.

"Girl, you alright?" Reign asked knowing how I felt. She was the only one I had shared my family secret with. She knew about the baby a while ago.

"Yeah, I'm good. I'm so sick of this hoe for real. What the fuck do she want from me?" I said getting all frustrated.

"Girl, if you would have listened to me a long time ago, we wouldn't be going through this shit," she said shaking her head.

"This isn't the time for the I told you so talk, Reign."

"Girl, I know. I'm sorry, it's just I hate this bitch just as much as you do. But baby, I know that hoe head ain't that fire. If so, I would def' pass on it."

"Oh, you better and it's def' fire," I said not believing I let her fuck me last night. "I know she just overreacting like any other bitch would. You know how we do when we got our feelings hurt," I said still justifying her actions.

"Nah, I can't agree. What happened to muthafuckas just busting out windows, keying cars, or slashin' tires?"

Later that day, I made a call that would surely get the ball rolling in my favor. By the time we showered, dressed and ate, we were out the door headed for our destination.

"Hit the block once then pull across the street in the vacant parking lot." Reign did as she was told.

"I see dude's car home. But he must haven't figured out we hit his ass yet? I don't know no nigga that got hit for a hunnid gees and decides to lay up in the bed until he sobers up. I mean, I know that was a helluva party. By the way, a party we didn't get to enjoy," said Reign.

"Trust me—the nigga in that bitch tryna sober up."

"Bitch, how you know?"

"Marc."

"So, you put that nigga on it? Damn, this world is full of crabs for real. His own boy?"

"Yeah, fuck all that."

"I wish you start lacing a bitch up."

"Girl, just chill," I said brushing her off. Just then, the drug task force swarmed the house that I used to live in.

"Bitch, are you kidding me? So, this is what you meant by eliminating our karma?"

"Yep and from the looks of it, that's exactly what's happening. He might not get convicted for Knowledge's murder, but I would be damned if he continues to live life freely. Hopefully, the nigga will get somebody to be his bitch and not the other way around. Maybe somebody can suck his dick in there."

We left Baton Rouge that day and I promised myself not ever to look back until I got my shit together. Right then and there, I knew I was going to a sobriety house. Oh, and let me not forget to abort this baby. I didn't want anything to tie me to Tony. I had gotten revenge for the death of my true soulmate. Now, hopefully, he could smile down on me and his soul may finally Rest In Peace.

Three Days and One Abortion Later

I thought I found the perfect time to try to kick this shit but each second that passed, made me feel I had made the biggest mistake of my life. Not only was this detoxing shit killing me, but I needed to snort a line bad. Everything I'd tried to consume only made my stomach more upset than it already was. I could never fully understand this inpatient shit. Going through this torture made me want to say fuck it.

"Come in!" I yelled when I heard knocking at the door.

It was the doctor this time and if looks could kill, someone would be planning his funeral. He definitely was not one of my favorite people.

"How are you feeling today, Ms. Cache?"

"I'm not doing so well, my body has been in extreme pain."

"When you are detoxing, the withdrawal experience can be really painful."

Did this nigga not know that I knew that shit already? "You don't know the half of it," I said grinding my teeth and clutching my stomach. I could feel myself about to vomit again. *Please God, help me!* I thought.

"Well, Ms. Cache, we've decided to give you Suboxone to help subdue some of the pain. After running a toxicology test, we not only found Cocaine in your system but traces of Heroin as well. That is the cause of your stomach and body aches. Before we do that, you have to promise to stop taking your IV out. We need to keep you hydrated and we don't need you any worse than you already are.

Heroin has never been my thang. The only way I can see it being in my system is from the X pills. I didn't care what it took to subdue the pain, I needed something.

"I promise, Doc. Now, hook me up and give me what you got," I agreed for him to shut up.

Shortly after getting me hooked back to the IV, I was in Suboxone heaven. I felt as if I had died and was enjoying peace on earth. Just that fast, I had forgotten about the excruciating pain and was ready to go. I felt as if I could do all things through Chr—naw, I quickly shook that thought out my head. I didn't want to make this biblical. In a rush, I packed everything I owned. I pulled out my phone and started dialing.

"Hello?"

"Yeah, come get me."

"You sure?" Reign asked not sure I was making the right choice.

"Yeah, I'm sure. I feel better, besides, this shit ain't for me." I also wanted to say, *I can kick this shit on my own.* But I decided against it. To be honest, I wasn't sure. I just had to take it one day at a time.

***

Cache

Reign came and picked me up within the hour. When she made it, all my shit was already packed.

"Bitch, you wasn't playing, huh?" She laughed.

"Shit no, this shit is overrated."

"Girl, it has only been a week, if that."

"Yeah, one long-ass week, besides, I know what I got to do."

"And what's that? Since you know it all."

"First thing, I gotta stay away from hoes like you." I laughed

"Bitch, please, if anything I'm that bitch."

"Yeah, you're right. You know I love yo' dog ass," I agreed.

"Bitch, I love you too. I just want what's best and fucking with that shit is far from it."

"I know." I hung my head low.

"So, look, what you want to do? Since we balling and shit."

That's why I fuck with her. The hoe had my back with whatever and as you can see, I trusted her with a hunnid thou.

"Fuck, to be honest, for right now, I don't want anything to do with the streets. I just want to lay up and pamper myself."

"What? You don't even want to hit the club? I can't believe that shit."

"Nah."

"I can't believe that shit, but if you like it, I love it. I been thinking 'bout it myself. This street shit is for the birds. I'm not sure what I'ma do with my money but I'ma invest. Maybe go to Hotlanta and try to get my kids back."

That came from left field. It's been so long since she spoke of her three kids. Sometimes I forget that she had them. About two years ago, she lost them to the system. She never really talked about it because she knew she fucked up and now she was feeling her mistakes.

"I'm proud of you." I touched her shoulder.

"Thanks." She hugged me.

Her kids' father used to beat her and their three kids. Almost going to jail for that shit, she had to testify in order to get her kids back. The State of Louisiana doesn't see the life of a poor black woman sometimes. All they see is the shoulda, coulda, wouldas. Sometimes a bitch's only way to cope is doing what she was taught and to survive to make it. She was scared to death of the nigga but what was she to do? Kill his no-good ass so she'd end up with a life sentence because the white man thinks the easy option is to walk away? To leave you in fear. I'm glad she is out of that situation. Hopefully, this money will help her do exactly what she needed.

"So, what you think, Cache? You coming or what?"

"Girl, I feel like you should go with yo' move. I'm giving you half of what I got. Fifty grand should do you good. Plus, when we get off the drugs and jewels, we will split that, too," I promised, knowing she could use it more than me. Three kids were a lot. "Whenever you get straight, I'ma come fuck with you. You already know that."

"The drugs I already sold. I'm meeting the buyer later today. I didn't want you to have to deal with that part knowing it is a possibility you would relapse or some shit. You know I got to protect my girl."

I had to admit, she most def' did that. I don't know where I would be if I could not call on her.

"Make yourself comfortable," she said once she opened her apartment door tossing the keys on the island. I'll pick you up a few things from you and Knowledge's place. With all you have been through, I know going back there will be tough."

"Thank you—for real," I said grabbing her hand. She just smiled and shook her head.

"I got some champagne if you want to drink a little and relax."

"Yeah, actually that sounds nice. I'ma shower first, though. I need to get this rehab smell off me."

"A'ight, while you do you, make yourself at home. I got to go make this run to meet up with this dude so I can get off this dope. The last thing I need is to get caught up with this shit." She kissed me on the top of my head and out the door she went.

CHAPTER 27

TONY

All this shit was a setup from the party to the threesome. I couldn't even remember how I got home. Everything after was a blur. When Cache was robbing me blind, I'm pretty sure that nigga Marc had something to do with it all, too. I had received a text from someone saying watch your bitch close with a picture attached of her coming out of the nigga's crib. I didn't even know she knew where he stayed.

"I'ma kill that bitch," I said out loud to no one in particular.

"Who you talking 'bout?" My cellmate asked

"Nigga, mind ya fucking business before I put ya head in the toilet." That must have gotten his punk ass mind right because he picked his book back up and continued to read. The book caught my eye. *When a Good Girl Goes Bad* by *Adrienne Johnson*. I knew that broad, she was from Gonzales, LA.

Word was she used to deal in Pharmaceuticals or some shit. She stayed getting popped for something but always beat the shit because it's all bogus. I respected the chick's hustle. You can't always believe the shit you hear through the streets. Them bitch niggas always speaking on somebody's downfall but never found the time to praise a nigga when they were up. That was the perfect example.

I walked out of my cell to go make a quick call. I dialed Cache first, no answer. I tried another number my right-hand CO.

"You have a collect call from, Tony. Pick up nigga—" Before the recording could, finish the call was accepted.

"What it do, my nigga?"

"Mane, I got knocked. I need you to come through with them racks." My nigga Corey always had my back.

"A'ight you know I'ma come through. Say no mo."

"You hear anything 'bout that hoe, Cache?" I asked tryna get the low down.

I hoped he could put two and two together. My dude wasn't stupid, though. He knew exactly what I was asking.

"Word on the street is a bitch named, Ray or Reign looking to get off a couple of keys for some houses," he spoke in code.

"Oh, yeah?" I said. "That's Cache's bitch. I need you to interfere if you catch my drift."

"0-4."

We both hung up and just like that I had put money on both of them hoes head. I just didn't understand why the fuck Cache would do this to a nigga? I hate that hoe. She has shown me bitches really can't be trusted.

Four hours passed before my name was called to pack my shit. I ran out that bitch like the floor was coming from under my feet. This shit was for the birds. Them the only muthafuckers that could come and leave as they pleased.

"What's up, homie?" CO asked smiling while dapping me down.

"Shit just wanted out that bitch. I hate being caged in, dog. The shit just isn't built for real niggas."

"Fucking right, you know I agree with that shit."

"You got a burner on you?"

"Shit yeah, here take this 45," he answered passing me something nasty.

"A'ight, cool, I got a lil piece of business to handle."

"That shit you asked me to do is as good as handled."

"Word?"

"Yeah, I'm on that shit as soon as the sun settles. The hoe just moving around till the clock runs out baby," he said lighting that good shit.

"What bout that hoe, Cache?"

"Mane that broad been ducked off. Niggas can't even spot her on the radar. But you know I got a team fulla hittas and them boys ready to put in work."

I shook my head to what he was saying, in deep thought. It's hard to believe that Cache would do something like this. I needed to talk to her. Yeah, I was burnt but some shit just wasn't right.

"When you catch up with her, bring her to me alive."

"Whatever you want my nigga." He passed the blunt.

We finally made it to my crib. All I needed to do was grab another gun and change into all black. I was 'bout to hit the streets hard. I needed to know what nigga balls was big enough to fuck with a nigga like me.

CHAPTER 28

REIGN

"Hello?" I answered my phone on the first ring knowing that no one else but Aaron could be calling. I sent him a text message earlier telling him, *//: The baker needs to get off these pies.* I hoped he understood what I was saying. The dudes that were supposed to come through days ago were stunting so I had to go a different route. Something in my gut told me not to fuck with the shit right off and to sit on it for a while. But I wanted to also get it off as soon as possible and not get caught up with this shit.

"Meet me halfway in Slidell," was all he said before he hung up.

I guess the nigga ain't want to talk over the phone as if my shit was tapped. I respected it, though. Before I left out my apartment, I grabbed my .22. This bitch might not be powerful but trust it would get the job done. Let a nigga try me.

I headed out the door letting Cache enjoy solitude. I just locked up and went on my merry way. Something in my gut told me to bring one of my niggas with me, but to many questions would be thrown out, sending up red flags. Too much was at stake. I already had too much up against me and if I let a nigga in on this, Aaron would be my last worry. Speaking from experience, muthafuckas from the NO are really cutthroat and I definitely didn't need any of that right now. As I pushed it down the highway, I listened to *Young Boy Never Broke Again.* By the time I made it to Slidell, Aaron was hitting me up.

"Sup?" I answered to see what was up.

"Meet me at the projects off Highway Eleven," he said.

"Alri—" Before I could finish, the nigga hung up the phone in my face once again. "Rude ass nigga, damn," I said but there was no reason to get all riled up.

I guess the nigga just didn't like talking over the phone considering the circumstances. I knew exactly where Aaron wanted to meet so I turned around and made my way to Stone Throw. It didn't take me long to pull into the parking lot. As soon as I spotted his car, I parked on the side of him in the empty space. I didn't know if we were meeting someone over here to make the sale or if this nigga wanted to purchase with me. The last thing I needed to do was get pulled over with a car full of drugs. I hoped whoever we were meeting over here was ready to do business. My kids mean more to me and I'm only a set away from having them back in my care. That is why I was glad to hit this lick with Cache. I needed the money. When this was all said and done, I was getting the fuck. I prayed that by then Cache would have her shit together too so she can could start over with me.

Finally, Aaron hopped out of the car with a duffle. Instead of getting in the front seat, he started walking toward the building. I followed suit leaving the bag. When I met up with Aaron in the stairwell of the project building, a dude accompanied him who introduced himself as CO. I tried keeping the look on my face straight, but I made sure to check this nigga on it. Neither one of us had agreed upon us having a third wheel. I did feel a lil skeptical. I tried catching eye contact with this nigga to try and read his facial expression, but his ass never could look me in the eye.

I had the .22 tucked safely in my back but I should've had that bitch clutched in my hand. Something just didn't feel right.

"You got the shit?" The nigga who called himself CO asked.

"Nigga, do you got the loot?" I shot back at him.

"Yeah, it's all here," he said tossing the duffle.

The next thing I hear are gunshots. I see a flash of light and everything goes back.

CO

Off the front seat, I grabbed the sack and ran back to my car hoping no one saw me. I had already taken my plates off so that was the least of my worries. I also knew these projects didn't have any cameras. I'd tied all loose ends. No witnesses, no case. I even slumped that nigga Aaron. He was a pussy nigga anyway. Right game, wrong nigga. Muthafuckas like him always caught the stand to save their own ass, sending real niggas like myself up the river. Like I always say, every, *i* must be dotted and *t* shall be crossed.

CHAPTER 29

TONY

"What you got?" I asked as soon as I answered the phone more enthused than I had been since all this shit happened.

"Everything is everything, my nigga."

"A'ight—" I went silent for a second, not because I was surprised but my heart never leads me wrong. That's why I always followed my shit. It was still too hard for me to believe the shit, but the evidence was in my face. What more could I ask for? "I got a hundon on both of them. Marc looking all spooked, right now but the nigga's clock should've been run out. As for Cache, bring her to me. She's pregnant with my seed so be careful my nigga. Muthafuckas all over town saying how she was out there down bad and shit on drugs. She must be in hiding. I'll give you half now and once the job's finished, I'll give you the rest." Without saying anything else, I hung up the phone, feeling infuriation.

I wanted everyone that was involved, including the stripper bitch. Everything inside me knew she was also in on the shit. Her and Cache came from the same kinda worlds, so she was also placed on my hit list. When I finish with her, she would wish she was dead. Like I said, getting back at all parties is a must. Niggas must have thought I was slipping. To be honest I had, because one thing I knew, you cannot turn a hoe into a housewife. Especially, a bitch named Cache.

CHAPTER 30

CACHE

When thou goest out to battle against thine enemies, and seest horses and chariots, and a people more than thou, be not afraid of them: for the Lord, thy God is with thee, which brought thee up out of the land of Egypt. Deuteronomy 20:1

Something in my soul kept bringing this scripture to my heart, but the devil also was on my shoulder telling me it was all lies. I'd been through so much shit that I didn't want to trust my heart. I also knew the devil comes to always kill, steal, and destroy. I believed if I held onto just a little hope, he would come like a thief in the night and snatch it away just as quick as it came.

When I looked up, I was back facing my demons and for the life of me, I couldn't understand why I would want a fix. I know I can beat this shit. I took out my Suboxone and placed a big chunk under my tongue. I pulled out my phone to call Reign once again but there was still no answer. I had started to worry because it was very unlike her to not pick up. My worst thoughts had started to kick in and I was a nervous wreck. I didn't know what else to do but wait by the phone to see if and when she would call.

Tony had been calling me nonstop so I'm assuming he must have jumped bond. He did make a few calls to me while he was locked up but those collect calls stopped. Now I was receiving calls straight from his line. I had reason to be worried. I knew when I first started fucking with him, he was a killer. I just thought I had the perfect plan to get away, but I guess I should've thought and planned this shit out a little more. I acted off emotions.

As for One, I hadn't heard or seen her in a while. I'm pretty sure her obsessive ass was too busy trying to win my family over. She was probably trying to come up with some shit to destroy my life more than she already has. To try to relax and get my mind off things, I turned all the lights off in the house and lit some scented candles. I ran me a nice hot bubble bath with scented bath beads.

I stripped out of my clothes and before I stepped inside, I turned on a little music to place me more in a relaxed mood. Once I was safely inside, I put my hair up above the tub so that it flowed outside without getting wet. I picked up the blunt and lighter that sat on the side of the tub, I lit it and inhaled deep. I was in a better mindset. I started drifting off, falling into a deep sleep.

***

CO aka COREY

The lights had finally gone off in the apartment I was keeping surveillance on. It was safe for me to make my move. I had been outside this muthafucka waiting long enough in this hot ass car. My fucking balls had starting sticking to the side of my legs. I pulled my Glock out checking the magazine and making sure I was fully loaded. I twisted the silencer on, safety off, and pulled the hammer back.

When I made it outside the door that I had been waiting to enter, I pulled the ski mask over my face. Twisting the doorknob to test my luck, I was surprised when I was able to gain entry.

The water had started getting cold and the Courvoisier bottle was empty. I got out of the tub to get a refill and to make freshwater. I used the light from the candle to feel my way around. I went to the kitchen to see what else I could sip on because all I wanted to do was drink all my sorrows away. Everything about my life was fucked up and at the moment, this bottle was my only escape.

I leaned out of the fridge and that when I felt a gloved hand around my mouth. I dropped the bottle, it shattered and splashed all over my feet.

“Don’t scream. Don’t run. I’m going to kill you if you do but listen to what I say and you live to see another day.”

I didn’t know who the fuck this was or what they wanted but I had to think quick. The nigga’s voice scared me more than anything. It sounded deadly like the dude off Taken when he was trying to get his daughter back. I thought fast, wasting no time kicking him in the nuts. I reached down to the floor next, picking a big piece of the bottle that laid on the floor. We both came up at the same time, but I sliced his face before he had a chance to react.

"You fucking bitch, I'ma kill you!"

I ran as fast as I could, grabbing my car keys on the way out the door. Behind me, I could see him pulling a gun from behind his back. Before I could get inside the car good enough, I had been shot in the back.

***

"Ayo, what's good?" Tony asked when he picked the phone up on the second ring. "Did you find her?"

"Mane yeah, I found that bitch and when I see her I'ma kill her ass?"

"Whoa, whoa, what the fuck happened?"

"Mane as soon as I had my hands on her ass, she kicked and cut me, man."

"What you mean? So, you let her get away?"

"Did you not hear what the fuck I just said?" I asked fuming.

"Look, I'ma let that shit slide this time nigga but all I need you to do is what I'm paying you for. Bring her to me alive."

I could tell this nigga was upset but fuck it. I'm worried 'bout my wellbeing. Fuck what ya heard. "A'ight," I said agreeing to his terms.

Before he could say anything else, I hung up. I was still pissed. I tucked my gun and hopped back into my car before the cops came.

CHAPTER 31

ONE

1:00 a.m.

The call I received from A'nett was unexpected. She called about 30 minutes ago telling me that MoMo C.W. had left out of the house, wandering the streets. She didn't know if she was sleepwalking at first or not. When we finally found her, she was at the burial site where Ann was laid to rest. At first, I thought she was just here because she missed her but when she came back to, she didn't even realize that she was there, or how she ended up there.

The way she kept going in and out, I knew what time it was. Her old age was coming down on her. When we made it back to her house, I called one of Ann's sisters to let her know what had happened. She was very surprised and quickly came over to see what was going on. A'nett told her aunt what had been going on lately but explained that today had been the first time that she had actually done anything like this. The poor baby. I had to shake my head at this shit. If only Cache knew how much she needed her mother. This only made me hate the bitch more but at the same time, I felt sorry for this family. That's why when Ann's sister Angela decided that they would take Mo-Mo C.W. back to their home but didn't know what to do with A'nett, I said I would look out for her. I told Angela I did not care how long I had to look out for her and that they can count on me.

"T.T?" A'nett called out to me once we were settled inside my home and not Cache's spot.

"Yeah, baby?" I asked

"I have something I want to talk to you about." She put her head down like something was really on her mind. I mean I understand her pain. She'd just lost her grandmother, who she thinks is her mother. Her great grandmother barely knows who she is half the time.

"Okay, you can talk to me about anything," I said giving her my undivided attention.

"One day I overheard my Grams talking to Cache. They were screaming and it scared me." She hung her head again.

I touched her shoulder letting her cry into my chest. "It's okay, baby. It's okay," I assured her.

"I know Cache is my mom. That's what she and MoMo C.W. were fussing about. Cache wanted to let me know the truth and MoMo C.W. refused her that right. I just don't understand why that's such a big secret. Some people must think Cache doesn't love me, but she does. I know she has been the reason I have always had the best of everything. Most people don't know that only the love of a mother is everything a girl could ask for."

To be honest, there was nothing I could say to top what she had already said. Right then and there, I knew I would protect this little girl with every breath that was left inside my body. That's why when I made up my mind to go through with the very last thing, I had up my sleeve for Cache, my heart was not heavy, nor would I regret what is sure to come.

I wiped my eyes because the tears wouldn't stop flowing. I thought about my own parents and how shit was so fucked up for me growing up. After tucking her in bed, I turned the lights out.

"Hello?" I answered my phone.

"This is Baton Rouge General Hospital. May I speak with a Maya Hidalgo."

"Yes, this is she," I responded wondering why the hospital was calling me this time of night. MoMo C.W. was at home with her daughter unless she got out again and got hurt.

"You were listed as Cache Price's emergency contact. She has been shot. We need you to come because the hospital is not sure if she will make it or not."

Now as bad as I wanted to get back at this hoe, this wasn't the way I wanted it all to end. The fact of me knowing A'Nett might lose her scared the hell out me. I looked back in on A'nett and she was still sound asleep. I grabbed my keys and hurried out of the house in the direction of Baton Rouge General Hospital.

CHAPTER 32

TONY

"What do you mean you think you shot her?" I asked CO not believing my fucking ears.

"I think I shot her, dog. The shit just happened. When she picked up the glass and sliced my face, I just lost it.

"Fuck! Do you know why I didn't want her harmed and brought back to me?" I asked him.

"To be honest my nigga, I don't have a clue. For one, you call me telling how the bitch hit you for over a hundred in cash and even more than that in dope. There's only one thing for a muthafucka to be calling me for. I kill muthafuckas, I'ma hitman, not no fucking babysitter, nigga."

"She pregnant with my seed," was all I could say before I grabbed my keys and headed out to Baton Rouge General.

***

Cache

Beep! Beep! Beep!

In the distance, I could hear a beeping noise and wasn't sure where that annoying sound was coming from. All I could remember was running for my life than feeling a burning sensation in my back that ripped through my stomach. I felt as if I was on cloud 9 and wasn't really sure if it all was a dream.

"When you go to war against your enemies, you might see that they have horses and chariots. They might even have an army stronger than yours. But don't be afraid of them. The Lord your God will be with you. After all, he brought you out of Egypt."

My eyes popped open. What I am doing here, in a hospital? It wasn't a dream.

***

One

"Yes, may I help you?" The nurse at the intake desk asked.

"Yeah, I'm here for a Cache Price."

"Hold for a second, please. Let me check which room she is in." Using a couple of strokes of the keyboard, she gave me her room number. I headed that way not really knowing what to expect. How would I feel or what I would do?

***

Now that I would finally be able to confront Cache about this pussy as shit she had pulled, I would be able to get to the bottom of this shit. I knew her and I just didn't see her doing no shit like this on her own. Maybe that nigga Marc put her up to all this. I needed answers but above all, I needed to make sure the baby was okay. I wouldn't be able to live with myself if something happened to my seed.

As soon as I pulled the door open, someone was in the room with her.

"Please don't hurt me anymore than you already have," Cache cried weakly.

Who the fuck was this bitch? That's when I realized it was the same bitch from the strip club. I went behind my back to get my burner.

"Cache Price?" Someone walked up behind me into the room. *Detectives.* "You are under arrest for the murder of Thadius Graham. You have the right to remain silent anything you say can be used against you in the court of law. If you cannot afford an attorney one would be appointed to you—"

As the two detectives cuffed Cache to the bed, the chick from the club walked backward out the door. As we locked eyes, I could see larceny in them and knew she was the piece to this puzzle. I never brought it up to Cache but when I did my background on her, I was told she was with a vicious bitch known as One and she wasn't to be trusted.

It was unspoken but the hoe knew the detectives had just saved her life. I hoped that she counted her blessings because the next time we crossed each other's path, someone had to die. I quickly made my exit before the cops could realize I was there to see Cache. I didn't need them to put me under a microscope.

I couldn't help it, but my mind flashed back to what the cops had said, "You are under arrest for the murder of Thadius Graham." Who the fuck was he and how the fuck did she get crossed up in a murder?

This shit just shows you never know who you're laid up with. I wondered if Cache and this bitch One had plans to rob and kill me? I guess the only thing for me is to find out and what better way for me to learn the facts than to turn to the streets.

CHAPTER 33

Eighteen Months Later

They say when it rains it pours. As I looked outside the mesh ironed window at freedom, I could not help but let these thoughts run through my mind. How in the fuck did I end up back incarcerated on a violent crime? This time though I was being held for a crime I did not commit. I had been charged with the murder of Thadius Graham in the first degree. At first, my mind could not imagine how could she have framed me for something I did not do. Sitting in here has made me think and the more I thought about it I came up with the answer. The night she had been at my house cleaning her gun as she always did, I made the mistake of picking it up, which had left my prints on it. She had been wearing gloves that night. *What a stupid mistake I had made costing me my life. This shit was not fair! I had the worst fucking luck,* I thought, shaking my head.

Did she not think I had suffered enough by her hands? She had taken everything from me including my daughter A'nett. The more I tried convincing my family that the bitch was Satan she would do what she does best, turn on her charm. Let's not forget showering my family with gifts and money making it rain as she has done for me on several occasions. Money being the motivator for my family get up and go it has always been easy to sway and dominate their asses.

As for Tony, the nigga was footing my incarceration bill. Paying for lawyers and everything else a bitch needed to keep up with the Kardashian in here. We were still not talking, that shit was on me. I still could not get over the fact he killed my first love, Knowledge. Muthafuckas might wonder why I still got the nigga on my team accepting that loochie from him if it's that's serious and if I hated him that much? That's the thing, just like my family, money over everything. What the fuck you mean? As you can see my pussy got to be worth more than a lil' bit. I hit his ass up over the head for over a hundred thousand, sent his ass to jail and still winning. Well minus this incarceration, shit but to my crazy ass ex, One is who I owe the standing ovation.

Anyhow back to what I was saying. Where was I? Yes, Tony, even though I got away with a grip from his ass, my friend, Reign lost more than either one of us. She lost her life. Now if you ask me was all this shit worth it? Fuck no. My girl was leaving all this reckless shit behind, turning over a new leaf and calling it quits. She'd planned to move to Atlanta after receiving full custody of her three kids, now that shit will never happen. I still held on to her half of the money. As soon as I can get my hands on it, I'ma pop Reign's mom off. Since Reign's looking down on all of us, her moms was granted full custody of the kids. I guess her losing her only daughter made her want to right all her wrongs between the two, with the stroke of a pen she was able to do just that. Praise God!

Speaking of praising God, the bullet wound I suffered by the hands of CO, Tony's homeboy, I must say I healed up nicely. Even though it will leave a nasty scar it won't be as bad as me losing the child I was pregnant with. At least that's the message I told my attorney to deliver to Tony. That was just my ugly strike. I wanted the nigga to feel bad for sending his goon behind me. He also was weak for me, so I milked the shit for what it was worth. That was all lies though I aborted his seed when I found the Cartier watch that I bought for Knowledge in Tony's makeshift safe. I did not feel the need to explain any of that shit to that nigga. He should know exactly why I did what I did. Fuck the fact that he got caught getting his dick sucked by my ex. I mean I could have looked past that, shit we could have both continued to bang her. I already had the hoe, not to his knowledge. He did not know I went into the relationship scoping him out.

One and I made our living off hitting these niggas across the head. We did not care if they were corner boys, kingpins, or white collar. My tender heart, happily ever after, loving ass had to go and give the nigga my heart instead of sticking to the plan. That only sent One over the edge, but my biggest mistake was not killing that hoe, Maya Hidalgo. I even owed Tony ass a hot slug. If I could take it all back, I would have used my last days on the street killing her with my bare hands or I would at least have tried. I would not have been soaking in the tub that night sipping out of a bottle like I was waiting to exhale.

Just know if and when this time is up, I will try my damnest to do exactly what these four walls been telling me to do, kill. Some might say fifteen years is not that long especially for murder but check this shit, I was not the one who pulled the fucking trigger! There or fucking not.

"Cache Price, attorney visit," the CO shouted from afar.

"Right on time," I said, hopping out the top bunk.

For me these days it did not take a bitch long to get ready for anything. MAC and designer clothes were all stripped away. The only thing I can do is get jailhouse ready. I took my orange jumpsuit from under my mat, making sure that my shit was nicely pressed righteously. After slipping inside it, I wet my hair and squeezed some Suave conditioner teasing my hair enough to give it that wet and wavy look. Thanks to Ann, my mother I could do that. To top my bad bitch prison look off, I wet my black pencil color with hot water and applied it like it was eyeliner. You learn to utilize all kinds of shit in here that you not even thinking twice about doing in the streets. Lastly, I cracked open my four-ounce jar of Vaseline and applied a touch to my luscious lips.

The things bitches do to look good, I thought to myself shaking my head.

"Price, let's go."

Right on time, I thought smiling while grabbing my manila folder with my important papers tucked safely inside.

I stood at the iron gate, manila folder under my arm with my hands sticking outside the slot waiting to be cuffed. Once I was safely secured, I stepped back while the guard signaled to the control center to pop my cell.

"Name and DOC," Sergeant Johnson asked looking on the clipboard as if he did not know me.

"Cache Price, 537855."

"A'ight keep to the right, Price and no talking."

I just stood there for a second with a look on my face that said nigga please are you fucking serious? But I did not object any more than giving him that look. I just did what I was told, I did not want to make a scene. This was neither the time nor the place. The walk to the attorney/client visitation was not long at all. It was right in the shakedown room, a place where I knew best. That was a whole 'other story. I stopped in front of the entrance while Sergeant Johnson opened the door for me to enter. When I stepped through, I was uncuffed and Johnson stepped out to guard the door, that is one advantage of the attorney/client privilege.

"Ms. Price, it is good to see you." Mr. Robert my attorney stood up showing a bitch a lil' respect. Something this era knew nothing about.

"Thank you," I said while he pulled my chair for me to sit. "You got my package?" I cut straight to it. No need to act all shy, I knew exactly what I wanted, and he did, too. I don't pretend, I never been that type of girl.

"Yeah, I do." He pulled it out the makeshift compartment of his briefcase.

Damn the poor man looked so nervous, it was hard for me not to laugh in his face. This is what his old, white ass was sweating me for, to Jose for me, so why not? Fuck it, it was not my fault he was lonely. That was him, he would rather be dedicated to his job than his wife.

Once he gave me the drugs that were rolled up airtight in the shape of a dick. I bust the orange jumpsuit open slipping it all into my wet vajayjay. I knew his perverted ass was looking at my clean-shaven fat, juicy, pussy and wanted a piece of this. So, you know what my nasty ass did, put on a lil' show for ass. Did or did he not deserve it? I mean I did have his law-abiding ass committing a crime for me. Smuggling drugs into a penal institution. I threw my head back moaning as if I could not fit the package inside of me.

"Fuck," I said under a whisper as if I was a damsel in distress.

"D—do you need help?" he asked stumbling over his words.

"Yes," I moaned as he stood up. "Wait, Robert, I got it," I said like I was out of breath but managed to push it inside. "Okay, where were we?" I smiled placing the tip of my finger in my mouth. I began to fix my clothes.

"Well, huh," he said, clearing his throat as if he was uncomfortable. "I have some papers for you that you would surely be happy to see. I went by your house to pick up your mail that you asked that was piled in your mailbox."

What the fuck's more important could be in my mailbox besides freedom papers? To his ass may be a reduction on his AARP card would make him happy, but for me getting out this muthafucka was the only thing that could make a bitch like me rejoice and shout.

"Here." He handed me an envelope that was light as a feather.

When I opened and unfolded the piece of paper, I never got to read it because the numbers popped out at me. Let me not forget the commas that went with the zeroes. I could have hit the floor. It was an insurance policy from an import/export company across the sea named Scott and Duncan. I never knew anything about this, maybe this was part of his retirement plan.

When I tell you, a bitch could have never been prepared for this. I could swear on the Bible that my heart stopped and skipped a beat for at least five seconds. Good thing it started back because a few more seconds I would have needed to be revived with a lil' mouth to mouth.

"So, what do you think Cache?" he asked, smiling like he had just hit the lotto.

I almost forgot he was in the room, the only person I was thinking about besides my kids was me, myself, and I. Fuck a nigga! Knowledge just proved to me that I did exactly what I was supposed to do toward Tony's ass! Fuck that nigga and his baby.

"I think I just need to get outta this bitch for one," I said standing up kissing him on the lips, shit I was excited. "Fucking right, that's what I think!" I almost shouted but decided against it. I did not want to draw too much attention.

"That is what else I needed to talk to you about." He hung his head down.

Without asking him what was on his mind I just waited until he decided to spit it out. I refused to let whatever he had to say bring me down. If I had to, I would do this fifteen-years on my head with no problem, money has always motivated me to do anything. He slid another white envelope over to me without saying anything else. Still, with a big cheesy ass smile on my face, I ripped that bitch opened with excitement thinking he was fucking with me and wanted to further surprise me once again.

Low and fucking behold, this is definitely what I was not expecting. I was being indicted on another murder charge, this time it was for the murder of my man, Knowledge Duncan. I'ma kill that bitch was my last thought before everything surrounding me went black.

CHAPTER 34

MAYA A.K.A ONE

After Cache got arrested for Thadius' murder, me almost catching a murder charge right in front of the arresting officers and Tony almost catching me slipping. I knew I had to get the fuck out of dodge. I also knew by the look on his face that he knew exactly who I was. I mean with the head game I put on his ass how could he forget me? I did not know where the nigga's thoughts were either and I didn't want to find out. Even with the cops that close, I still did not want to turn my head the other way. Just in case he wanted to start bustin' I was ready for whatever. For it to be me or him. Shit, I did not know the nigga from a can of paint. So, what if I had the nigga dick down my throat? Who was he again? The muthafucka I planned to put a bullet in his head as soon as I came from my vacation. I even had a special bullet with the nigga's name on it. Just to let the nigga know I ain't the one to be fucked up.

As soon as I reconnect with my grandfather Mexican Cartel Boss Emilio Hidalgo. I even brought A'Nett with me since I am her legal guardian. I found out sooner rather than later she is definitely her mother's daughter. For the right price, she left everything behind pretending to be my seed. She is a true hustler, it was a front for her now great grandfather. It is a good thing Cache's ass has a good grain of hair and her skin tone looked a lil mocha with a dash of cream. If Emilio found out the shit, I was trying to pull was a lie, me and poor A'nett's ass would be floating up the Panucho River.

I told A'nett from now on until further notice she would go by Emilia as if I had named her after my mother, her grandmother.

"Ms. Hidalgo." I heard a knock at the door and my name being called. "Your driver is here," Miguel the house servant aka the hitman, said through the door.

I remembered him clearly from my short-lived childhood when I lived here.

"Emilia, are you ready?' I asked her, while she was obviously on social media. That child acted as if her phone was embedded inside her DNA. "Emilia, did you hear me?" I said a little sterner to make sure she heard me and most importantly to not forget her new name.

"Yes," she finally answered jerking her head up from the screen.

"A'ight, let's go then. Mami."

"Hola, Mr. Miguel," A'nett said when we stepped out of our assigned quarters.

This damn girl was too smart for her own good. She knew a little Spanish now thanks to the homeschooling she was being taught by Maria.

"Si, Ms. Emilia." He smiled. "How did you ladies sleep last night?"

"Perfecto," A'nett responded politely.

She looked like an angel in her all-white linen Alexander McQueen summer dress with gold accessories. She wore her hair down, flowing past her shoulders with a middle part.

"Good," he said, before walking in the opposite direction.

When we made it outside of the beautifully equipped compound the sun shined brightly in our faces. A driver was waiting with the door open for our arrival. He looked very vicious in his tailor-made Armani suit with loafers to match. I could not tell by his baby face but the look in his eyes said that he was a stone, cold-blooded killer. He had that same faraway look that I tried to hide but it is not that easy to camouflage when you are looking at your own kind. What is that saying? Birds of a feather flock together.

Once we were all tucked safely inside the bulletproof vehicle, I popped open a bottle of bubbly and sipped from a flute while I looked out at my beautiful birthplace. I barely remembered this place, but the people and quiet made me adore it and want to stay forever. Here I felt like I did not need anyone to love me because here I was learning to love myself. But of course, with time I will get there. It might seem cowardice of me to run away and not squash the beef I adopted through Cache's ass. In due time, though, I will. I just needed to rejuvenate my inner self.

I had started to get a lil' sloppy and it was clearly proven when I ran up on Cache in the hospital. I could have and would have lost my life if it was not for the detectives rolling up when they did. I had some shit for the both of them just because this nigga Tony loved my bitch harder than I ever I could, I couldn't let that go.

"What are we doing today?" A'nett asked.

"We are about to hit the spa lil' momma, show you how I do shit." I smiled knowing she would like our outing.

Once we made it to our destination, thirty minutes later, we waited until our driver came to open the door to step out. When we first got there A'nett, of course, wasn't used to being treated righteously. Fuck I was not used to being treated like a Mafia princess, but I could definitely get used to this shit.

"Gracias," I said stepping out onto the pavement, red bottoms first with A'nett following close behind with her face still buried in the phone. These days everyone loves social media, even the kids.

As we stepped inside the beautifully decorated spa, we were surrounded in seconds. Anytime you stepped in a foreign place and was considered an American, shit like this happened. The workers flocked to get that American dollar, that dinero.

"Good afternoon ladies," a short chunky lady greeted us as soon as she could. "How may we be of your service?" She offered all three of us a flute of Champagne.

Our escort denied the offer, but I allowed A'nett just one glass. They knew Emilio was my grandfather and the city of Guadalajara respected his gangsta. My grandfather put a lot of money in this godforsaken place and if it was not for him a lot of muthafuckas would not eat. That said the place had been shut down for us because Emilio broke bread with the poor. I was told that is something to expect everywhere I go while in Mexico. Like I said a bitch could definitely get used to a muthafucka waiting on me hand and foot.

After letting her know we wanted the full package, we went into separate rooms to change into robes. I knew A'nett would appreciate some shit like this. The baby deserved it. I watched her as she walked off and notice how she was blossoming into a young lady over the year and a half she'd been with me. She really has seen too much at such a young age. I hope Cache's ass is rotting in that fucking jail cell. She did not deserve to be a mother. Fuck she had never been there for either of her kids. She had slowly begun to let the streets suck her up just like her mother Ann. God bless the dead.

Once we were in our white, plush robes, we laid back in the recliner chairs for our facial masks while also soaking our feet.

"How are you feeling?' I asked A'nett, smiling knowing she was enjoying herself.

"I'm loving it. I never been on a vacay and on top of that a five-star spa. So, yes I'm really feeling myself. You know I had to tweet this." She smiled showing her dimples that she inherited from her late grandmother, Ann.

I also did not mind her posting on social media even though we are scheming and hiding. She knew not to mention nothing about her old family. As for that nigga Tony? The nigga's money or respect could not touch Emilio's, so I was not worried about his ass touching a hair on my body. My grandfather had around the clock protection and I doubt Tony would make it past the sharpshooters. I knew without a doubt the army of goons was touching anything that poses as a threat.

Before the cucumbers were on my eyes my phone started. I slid my thumb across my phone screen for my fingerprints to unlock it.

"The fuck?" I said under my breath.

"What?" A'nett asked, concerned.

"Nothing," I responded, never taking my eyes off the screen. Someone had sent a message from a blocked number.

//: You are a dead bitch the next time I see you and trust me our paths will cross.

Someone had to be playing a trick on me. I looked over at A'nett, she had plugged her music back into her ears. I looked over at our driver and he was still standing by the door guarding it with his life. Fuck it, I knew I was protected no matter who was out lurking. Besides, I had too many muthafuckas to worry about. If I tried to count on my fingers and toes the people that had beef with me I would run out of them. But just in case Cache's ass is thinking she cannot be touched I decided to send a message and prove she was clearly wrong about my reach.

CHAPTER 35

CACHE

I had finally built up the courage to call Tony. I just hoped that he could forgive me. Once again, this bitch found a way to get to me. I hated this hoe for making me love her the way that I did, for loving her at all. What did I do to her that made her hate me so much? She gave me plenty of reasons to feel the way I do, with her I just don't get it. Her coming back into my life has always been ill-intended.

I did not need anyone to tell me that she had killed Knowledge, fuck I didn't even need her to confess to the shit. It was in black and white and black and white don't lie, after reading over the indictment for the murder of Knowledge Duncan. I knew now that the skank hoe had started all this fucked up ass shit that's been coming down on my life. As I said black and white don't lie ballistics had found a match between the two murders.

"Ayo, Cache, you good?" one of my fellow inmates named Killa asked passing by my cell.

"Yeah, everything is everything." She passed me a slip of paper and walked off.

Of course, she was not asking about the lil' episode that happened today in the lawyer's conference. I pulled out my flip phone. Having a phone period in jail, you was doing it big. I definitely did not need anything more than what I have. I dialed the number on the paper to make sure the money was placed on the green dot card, it was. Not trusting a soul in or out this bitch I transferred the money to my outside account. It would have been nothing for a girl to go back and take the money off the card herself.

I'd rather be safe than sorry. Even though I found out Knowledge left me with a nice bag, hustling would always be in my blood. I was not about to stop because I had it either. Then on top of all that, these doped out ass hoes will pay the max to get high or die trying. On the streets, a strip would go for ten dollars no more than fifteen. In here, I was running them bitches three hundred a head. I loved dealing with Killa, she had this white bitch. Them the ones with the best suga daddies. Them old white crackers stuck around even when them hoes catch a life sentence.

I know one chick killed her suga daddy's disabled mother. I could not believe his ass caught the stand, put his right hand on the Bible swearing she was with him. When they said white people stick together, they were not fibbing. Niggas really down bad though, they gone before a bitch could feel the coolness from the cuffs. I just didn't get the shit. That was one reason I vowed to never love anyone but Knowledge and Tony was a different story.

After making myself a sale, I tried Tony's number once again, no answer. He had to be handling business and could not make it to the phone.

"I will just text, fuck it," I said aloud. Now that I knew what I knew, I knew that I could get out of this bitch. All the DA would have to do is check the cell towers and it will tell the truth.

My location at the time with both shootings. Thank God we did not have our phones on us the day Thadius Graham was murdered. Robert did not know the time frame of the process, but I told him I don't give a fuck what he had to do. All I wanted from him was to make the shit happen. I didn't give a fuck if he had to go play golf or suck the judge's dick. Whatever it took to get me out of this hell hole was fine with me. I told Robert to do was to make it work and as soon as possible.

Exhausted and feeling a little fatigued from today's good and bad news I decided to lay it down for a little while. First, I wanted to shower and release some stress. Before grabbing my shower bag with my clothes and personals, I slipped on my robe and shower slippers. We did not have much privacy, so I had to get fully undressed in front of my cellmate. I was not tripping on that shit I got used to it and yes it was very different from undressing for money. Without missing a beat, I headed straight for the shower.

As always on my way, I listened to music. I had a touch screen tablet, provided through J-Pay. I listened to my Beyoncé album *Dangerously in Love*. I was all in my feelings from finding out that lil' piece of business about Tony. It was hard to accept that the nigga didn't double-cross me. Had me falling for this nigga once again. I know I fucked up, I did him wrong and instead of sitting down like two adults, I may have overreacted, especially when I saw the watch of my now-dead boyfriend. I don't know how she did it.

"All that is hidden in the dark will surely come to light," My grandmother MoMo C.W.'s words spoke loudly to me. I should have seen all the signs but were there really any signs for me to be cautious about?

Finally making it to the showers at my usual time there was not a soul in sight, which is how I preferred it. Like a ghost town, I loved the solitude at this hour of the day. This was the only time I had just an ounce of privacy. It was very hard to find any of that around a place like this. I stood under the water after adjusting it to what my body could stand. I let the water beat down on my head only to flow freely down my body touching every curve.

My mind started taking a trip back down memory lane. I thought about the past and how I used to always use the streets as my refuge, especially when I needed life to make sense, but nothing other than that I could relate to. If I went on a different path and decided to do anything better with my life, I would not be where I am. Maybe on the other side of the law, I'm not that type of girl, though. However, just as they say, you can take a girl out of the hood, but you can not take the hood out of a girl.

I have not prayed in years, but this is definitely a time I should hit my knees because I pray to God, the next time I see that two-headed snake ass bitch, I plan to do my best to leave her right where she stands. It is too late for us to have a sit-down. We're past any of that talking bullshit. I let this hoe cross a line that she should never have. Besides I am tired of just bowing down to this bitch like she owns me. Fuck, if she did not know she definitely made an enemy for life.

As I continued to let the water run, I picked up my soap to wash my face. That's when the lights went out and someone grabbed me from behind. I start to scream but a hand put a vice grip over my mouth knocking my scream right back down. It was big enough to cover half of my face. I thought the worst I was about to get raped. I always felt a few lustful eyes roaming over my body by the men that worked here. They knew my rep from the strip club, a few of them anyway. I was not fucking with any of them though except Sergeant Johnson. Of course, I had to pop him off properly for coming through when I need him to be front and center but taking a bitch's goodies was unjustifiable.

I thrashed, kicked and scratched, but the arms held me tightly and wasn't letting up. I finally found a way to bite one of the fingers.

"Fucking bitch," a rough voice cried out. These were women, not men!

"Damn, shut the fuck up and keep this bitch mouth covered."

At that moment I ran every face and voice through my mind who I had ever come in contact with. To see if I knew who could have been out for me, nothing came up. I don't know anyone in here that would want to do me any harm unless they were coming for drugs, but I was not stupid to keep that shit on me.

Something black had been thrown over my head and my hands were quickly tied behind my back. I struggled to breathe, I had no clue what these hoes plans for me were. I never did time before and thus I stayed away from shit like this. I also did not have a crew in this bitch for protection. So, I should have been prepared. I should have known these hoes would be gunning for me. Never thought I would need one, in a fair fight, I can hold my own shit. As I have said plenty of times before there is no honor amongst thieves. Wrong muthafuckin' place for me to ever get comfortable, right?

I quickly evaluated the situation. Three people, one to my left, one to my right and the last one behind me. Just when I thought I was prepared for what was to come next, my back smacks to the wet floor from the punch I received from the aggressor to my left.

"Bitch, you can't hit harder than that?" I said mocking her.

I would have been laughing if my shit was not covered. The only reason I fell was because of the wet floor and these non-slick resistant shower shoes, she knew that shit, too.

"You know what? Let's stop playing with this bitch. I don't have all day."

That's when a pain shoots up my jaw and spreads across my face. I knew that had to be delivered from the big handed person that grabbed me. If this sack wasn't over my face, I knew my vision would be blurry. My eyes started ringing and I began to get dizzy. I was off-balance from the rain of punches that connected with my head. I don't remember how, but someway I ended back on my feet, hands still tied behind my back. The best thing I could have been doing at that moment would have been to lay in the fetal position, but my mind would not allow me, I am a fighter.

On my feet, on my feet, don't fall. I kept mentally coaching myself. That's when I felt a size twelve-foot kick me hard in my stomach, knocking the air out of my lungs. I could not breathe.

"Maya sends her regards, bitch," she said before spitting on me and walking off.

I felt as if she had kicked every ounce of strength I had left and that's when everything went completely black.

CHAPTER 36

ANTONIO *TONY* CLARK

When I finished handling my business, I checked my phone to see if I had any missed calls. I did, a few actually, but the only one that caught my attention was the two I missed from Cache. "Fuck," I said banging my hand on the steering wheel. I had been waiting on this fucking call for over a year now. Now that it finally came and I missed it.

***

The night was still young, so me and my nigga CO decided to celebrate. The meeting that I had earlier in the day had gone smooth. So, yeah, I definitely had something to toast to. I told CO that we should relax because after a while shit was about to change for the better. I had found a connect that had straight fish scale for the low-low. I had no other choice but to jump on the banana boat with the discount prices I had gotten. Life for me soon would be better than I could have ever imagined.

Once we pulled up to the club in our fly ass whips, we bypassed the long line and went straight to the door to enter the club. The whole crew was dressed in all black looking like the mob. This was how we rolled every time we went out together. No one dared speak a word to us either. Some might say that we lived by intimidation but how I looked at it with our vicious demeanor just demanded respect.

The deal I made today is only going to place me on a higher scale. The only thing is, I still had this court shit hanging over my head and I had to make sure I walked lightly. I made a mental note to make sure to call my lawyer, Robert to see if his ass had this shit taken care of. I'm paying him too much money for this shit to still be an issue. Shit been really good for me, so it only makes me confident that everything else in my life will fall in place.

After all of us had taken our spot and got comfortable in the VIP section, I took in the scene just to get familiar with the streets. Anybody who was somebody hung out here. This is why the streets really talked maybe not verbally but all you had to do was sit back and take it all in stride. Who had the best cars, the most jewelry, watch the ones that bought the bar out, the biggest fan club and the important one of all is the nigga with the most hoes on his dick. Where there is real money, the hoes were not too far away and there is your greatest competition. As long as I keep the upper hand and not lose sight of what I originally got in this shit for. I can easily line my competition up knocking them down with no effort.

As the night eased by the club grew more anxious you would have thought shit would have died down by now, but it was only just the beginning. Muthafuckas was in this bitch wildn' out. Their actions were expected, though. Anytime you had a room full of black folks there is almost always chaos. There was no need for drugs or Cognac to make them act like animals. I was not complaining though because if every nigga was like me the murder rate would be ferocious. I did not play 'bout my money and as I said if I had ever found my match the nigga would have to go. I didn't need another me out lurking for the same kinda money bag I was tryna kidnap.

The sight was beautiful on my side with my niggas, though, shit was lovely. Each time we linked it was always a celebration and as long as me and my team was eating, I was good.

"Ayo, my nigga. Come get you a drink or something, enjoy yourself," CO said drunkenly, throwing his arm around me, more for support, I could tell he had a lil' too much to drink.

"I'm good, my nigga, besides I haven't even finished with my first drink."

"Mane you need to loosen up, my dude you surrounded by family. Besides, that shit you drinking watered down." He tried to smile but the scar Cache left on his face did not allow him to do that, at least on one side of his face.

Ever since the shit happened the nigga been having one too many drinks. I felt bad because I knew the nigga took pride in his appearance.

"A'ight, you right. I'm going to have another drink but who the fuck gon' be the designated driver when all you fools too drunk to even know where ya dicks at? You know they slick slide loving the crew. So, you know I'm trying to be on my double-O-seven when shit rang out."

"Cool as long as I know my nigga got me I am untouchable, right?' he said as we walked off in union.

I had to smile and shake my head at Corey, cuz my boy can be sloppy when he found himself in a pool of liquor. The nigga was right about one thing, though, I definitely had his back.

"Nigga, watch where the fuck you going," some off-brand nigga said bumping into CO.

"Bitch, fuck you broke ass nigga."

Before I knew it, CO had sobered up quick, punching dude dead in the face making him stumble.

"Try it if you want, nigga and within the week ya momma will be left raising money for yo' final resting place," I said drawing down on his weak ass. Security came over asap, but I wasn't worried about them.

"Whoa, whoa, Y'all chill," The nigga said, realizing who I was and knew I wouldn't hesitate to shoot this nigga and then turn the gun on him. "Take this nigga out, mane before shit turns sour," he said knowing how I get down. "My nigga, you good?" I just looked at that nigga and walked off with CO not saying shit.

I realized that I just almost caught a hat charge in front of a thousand witnesses. For my nigga, I would take that lick.

***

When we exited the club, I knew from the color of the moon that the sun was not too far behind. I did end up having one too many drinks but not enough to not be alert. Everyone was doing their own thing, either leaving the club with their boys or trying to leave with a different flavor of their choice of pussy for the night.

I heard gunshots out of the blue that made me whip my head in the direction from which they came. That's when I see my nigga's CO facial expression go stiff like he was stuck in time. Like someone had hit pause on his life. He fell to his knees and his arms went limp at his sides and that was when I knew that I would never see my nigga again. During all the commotion and the stampede of frantic people, I was still able to zero in on the person taking off with the black hoodie over his head. I pulled out my gun again for the second time that night but this time I sent shots without thinking. I sent them bitches his way with no regard. I could tell he was hit, I just hoped it was a deadly shot.

When the nigga in all black hit the side of the building in the distance I could hear the sound of the police siren. That shit snapped me back to reality with the quickness. Besides thinking about the dope charge I already had hanging over my head. I thought about these crooked ass cops. I knew I had to get the fuck out. I thought about my family holding a press conference for my death committed by another white cop only for them to get placed on suspension with pay! Later, my dismissal by a trigger-happy cop would be ruled as justified. That's how that shit goes, especially when a nigga gets shot with his back turned? Or get shot down without posing as a threat? I just did not get that shit.

I got the fuck on though cuz I refused to be caught on a funny style. I had to accept this as of now but when the time comes, and this shit comes to the surface I am definitely popping a nigga's head. I hated to leave CO just laid out there slaughtered like a piece of meat, but I needed to get out of there before something happened that I would regret.

CHAPTER 37

CACHE

When I woke up, I did not feel much, my head did feel a little fuzzy, but other than that, no pain. I'm assuming the IV drip I was connected to was the reason.

"I see you finally woke up?" I heard from the left side of me.

I opened one eye, the other stayed shut as if it was glued together. Standing over me to the right was Nurse Brown. She had been working in the jail infirmary for years and what I was told she treated everyone in here with care, kindness, and love. So, even though I was paranoid about my surroundings I did not have to worry about if One had somehow gotten to Nurse Brown to put something in my IV drip that would kill me. All I knew is I needed to get out of here as soon as possible. People always thought behind bars was safe, but I was too exposed. I would not dare complain about it, though, protective custody was out of the question.

"Are you ready to tell me the truth about what happened to you?" Nurse Brown asked in her sweet, concerned voice.

"All I remember was tripping and falling. Everything after that is a blur. I must have knocked my head on something on my way down. You know how slippery those shower slippers can be."

"Yeah, I agree. You must have slipped and bumped your head on something if you think I believe any of that bullshit coming out of your mouth."

Damn, I thought, shaking my head I could not get nothing past her.

"I know how rowdy these girls can be in here. I been down over twenty years, so I have seen a lot." She smiled. "But you, Ms. Cache. Indeed, I know you got good in you somewhere. I watch you all the time, you don't go putting your nose where it don't belong, smelling other people's shit. So, chile, you can go tell them lies to someone else without ears, eyes, and most importantly, common sense. Trust me when I say I been round the block a time or two."

“Believe what you want Nurse Brown, but if you think I’m ‘bout to let y’all hold me up in solitary confinement I will die before I go be held like a hostage. This is enough locked up for me for a lifetime.”

“Mmmm, I hear you, chile. What is the rate of your pain on a scale of one through ten?”

“Twenty,” I answered ready to go back to sleep.

She walked off without saying nothing. I know she could read through my bullshit. Shit, I did not give a fuck. A few minutes later she came back with a little small paper cup and a plastic cup filled with water.

“Here,” she said dumping the pills in my hand and giving me the cup.

After throwing the tablets back I drunk all the water to flush them down. She waited on me to open my mouth to double-check to see if I had swallowed them.

“Get you some rest because it is apparent you need it.” She walked out of the room without saying anything else.

***

The next time I opened my eyes I smelled dirt coffee that is served from the kitchen. It was breakfast time. I got up to wash my face and brush my teeth before the infirmary orderly made it on my side to serve. I usually didn’t eat the shit that was served in the kitchen but if I didn’t put something inside my stomach all the pills, I have been taking will have me worst off. I tried getting out the bed but today the pain was another story. It was a constant throb in my head and my ribs. The pain was horrifying and I should not have moved anything because it would only make it worse. I got up anyway though no need for me to pretend I’m half dead. I only felt that way.

When I finally did make it out of the bed, I stood there for a second or two. I made it to the mirror wanting to get a good look at my reflection. I did not help that I could only see out of one eye and on top of that the mirrors sucked. From what I did see, I looked horrible. I had to pay these bitches back whoever did this to me. All I had to do was find the bitch with the biggest feet and I had the crew that fucked over me.

I was not afraid of whoever these hoes were but I would play possum. I needed these bitches to think I am weak. I had to pretend to be vulnerable, so when I strike back no one would ever expect little ole me.

Once the food came around the orderly gave me my tray with a cup of orange juice, I don't fuck with the kitchen coffee so I declined. I went back to my bed to see what hells kitchen had decided to serve today. I just hoped it was something I could put on my stomach until I get out of this bitch today. To my surprise, someone had hooked me up. Buttery biscuits, creamy grits, fluffy eggs, and a slice of real ham burnt around the edges just how I like, I dug in.

Even eating hurt, but the shit was too delicious to stop. Since I been down, I been living off canteen and my favorite thing to eat at home is breakfast. Plus, it is the most important meal of the day. I picked my biscuit up about to slaughter it, then I noticed that under it was a letter wrapped in plastic. What the fuck? They said don't take the chips. They failed to mention anything about a state tray.

Curiosity killed the cat, you know I did not stand a chance. I opened it up to read it, on some shit I was spooked because now I felt like somebody was trying to poison me.

I know who did that shit to you come see me once you get out. Look for teardrops and you will find me. Hope you enjoyed your breakfast.

Still not knowing who wrote this shit, I decided I had enough food. I am pretty sure I will soon find out, all I had to do was look for teardrops. I did not know if this shit was another trap or not, but like I said curiosity is what killed the cat.

CHAPTER 38

TONY

Only a few days had drifted by since CO was murdered. I put a couple of hundreds out on any accurate information that would lead me to the muthafucka that bodied my nigga. Since this shit happened my head been fucked up. Had me wondering who could have possibly done this. I had to find out who this nigga was I pulled out on in the club. I fucked up. Everybody in our crew was over at my crib getting ready to go to his funeral, including some of his immediate family. I paid for everything from the clothes to his final resting place. I also put the lil' program together because his momma and wife didn't have the strength to do it. My nigga would not have wanted it any other way, so like he would have for me, I had to show up and show out. I also plan to pop them both off with a nice chunk of change to hold them over. CO had always been the breadwinner of his family, so I knew they would need it to make ends meet. Even though I knew CO would truly be missed I just hoped his family understood this is the life he wanted.

"You in there?" I heard Toya, CO's wife knocking on the door. "The family car is parked out front waiting for us."

I took the last swig of my drink, stood in front of the mirror to make sure my attire was well put together and headed out the door. It was time to lay my nigga to rest.

***

After we all celebrated the life of Corey Jackson, we had all got drunk, well excluding me. Really not much of a drinker when I needed a clear head. I let everyone else do they shit. I was knee-deep in the game to cop out now. I just needed to roll with the hand I had been dealt and pray I could move on to better things.

Tomorrow after I stop in to see my lawyer, I was to head out as soon as possible. I needed to make sure my package touched down safely. Now that CO was gone, I did not trust another nigga to oversee my day to day business. I did have foot soldiers that I trusted but that was only a guarantee to knock a nigga off and to hold the block down.

I was sitting, smoking a blunt and clearing my head on the back patio when my phone vibrated letting me know that someone was trying to get in touch with me. I looked down to see who it could be. I was tired of muthafuckas hitting me up with false info on the nigga who did this to CO. It seemed like everybody and their momma was out to get this money. To my surprise, it was my baby texting me.

//: Can you talk?

//: Fucking right.

Soon as she must have gotten my text, she hit me back asap.

"What's good, you alright?" I asked, concerned because hearing from her was some shit I was not used to anymore.

"Yeah, I am okay. I just want to say I'm sorry and I hope you can forgive me."

I could hear tears in her voice, and I knew they were falling freely from her eyes.

"We good, Cache. You should already know that" I said, letting my heart talk. "I just need you to explain to me why would you do a nigga like that? I ain't been nothing but good to you. I gave you my heart, ma."

"That's exactly what I wanted to speak with you about."

I did not say nothing, I just listened to what she had to say.

"I'm not really sure how to say this, but the girl you was in the VIP section having sex with, was my ex."

"Actually, I would not call it sex. The bitch just sucked my dick," I said, feeling a little salty. "Did you set the shit up? I always heard through the streets about two heartless bitches setting niggas up. I just never put you to be associated with the shit. Now I get it." Realizing I was a target from jump, she never loved a nigga and I should have seen that shit.

"No, I mean yeah. You were a target, but I ended up falling in love with you. That shit in the VIP was all her doing. When I came in and saw y'all that shit really fucked my head up at first. I had been stopped fucking with her. You got to believe me," she pleaded her case.

"So, why did you fuck both of us that night?" I asked, searching for answers that were overdue.

"Because I knew that is what she wanted, and I did not need her to expose the truth. I knew if she did you would not be capable of ever loving or forgiving me."

"That ain't how that shit go, ma. Not in the real world," I said shaking my head as if she was there, not believing the shit she was saying. I mean the fuck.

"Don't fucking judge me, Tony! There is no difference from the way I used to hustle than the way you do yo' dirt. Only I am not fighting over a block. I let you niggas do it, I just want a piece of the pie. Muthafuckas like you make it hard to respect what you do. When all y'all do is look at a bitch like a fuck."

"Understood, but if you changed yo' mind 'bout me why you still hit a nigga's pockets?" I just did not get where she was going with this. If you asked me, she was taking a nigga in circles.

"One must have—"

"Who the fuck is One and what the fuck they have to do with what I'm asking?" I asked confused.

"My ex Maya, she must have planted my child's father's watch in your safe trying to frame you for it."

"What watch?" I asked because none of this shit made sense.

"A Cartier watch that I bought him."

As Cache continued to explain everything to me, I still felt it hard to believe. This shit was a hard pill to swallow. No lie I did respect her hustle. I might not like it, but I had no choice but to respect it. By the time she finished running the shit down to me, all that shit had me wondering could she have had CO touched.

"When the last time you talk to the bitch?" I asked.

"The night I got arrested."

She might have, shit, can I trust her. I could tell she avoided saying the night she got shot. That was a sensitive subject for both of us. I wasn't sure if I should mention CO to her. I doubt whoever this hoe Maya or One whatever she called herself had that much pull or was she that bold? Then again Cache just proved to me you can not trust a pretty face. Them hoes are the deadliest.

Before we disconnected the phone, I had to let her know to give me time to think. I needed a few days. My mind was clearly still all over the place because even though my mind was telling me to leave Cache's ass to rot, my heart told a whole 'other story. I just had to keep flipping through each chapter and see how our story would end. I hadn't done anything more but love this broad. Now don't get me wrong I have done my fair share of bullshit, but nothing compared to this. As of now, I did not need any distractions and I decided to deal with this shit later. I know one thing for sure, she definitely gave me a lot to think about.

CHAPTER 39

CACHE

I did not know what to expect after talking to Tony. I just needed him to forgive me. I realized that I fucked up. I made a mistake all because of this hoe, One. The tables had definitely turned, she had become prey and I the predator. How did I allow her to pull a rabbit out of a hat on me? I didn't expect any of this. Shit, not even the fact that she had that much power to get a bitch's attention in here. Let's not forget CO, that shit had her name all over it. I just could not bring it up to Tony that would only give him more reason to hate me.

I was not safe in here or anywhere else, but at least I would be able to stand up to this bitch if I was home. I deserved a fair fight with her. Now that I knew I was dealing with a snake, I had to chop this hoe's head off. It was easier for me knowing what I am up against. Back then I was so blind to see what was right before my eyes. I could not see she controlled the strings behind this puppet.

I pulled out my pictures and searched for the pictures of my kids. Everything good I have ever set my mind to was because of them but the devil somehow always robbed me of my good intentions. I knew what had to be done if I could not beat her, I had to join her, it was time that I got even. I had to get just as grimy as she could be, even grimier.

"Mail call!" the C.O. in the control center shouted popping all the cell doors open just in case they were locked in.

"Ashley Stewart, Latoya Woods, Markal Johnson, Miracle Moore, Cache Price."

My name had been called, which was unexpected. I usually get my mail on the kiosk, unless my mother in law writes and sends pictures. She wasn't in tune with technology. She could not respect what social media was used for. She always said it was used for more than communication and it caused too much trouble. Even Snapchat, even though it erased the stuff could still be traced.

"Cache Price," I said showing my ID.

"Here," she said, handing me two envelopes. "And step to the side, you have legal mail."

I did as I was told and waited patiently until she opted to finish. I felt like I was being watched. I looked around the dayroom, trying my best to not make it noticeable. I didn't see no one looking my way. Maybe I was tripping with all the shit that has happened to me. Not seeing anyone watching, as I waited, I opened my mail. To my surprise it was A'nett. I closed it back up with a smile on my face I was going to read it once I got back into my cell.

"Come on, Price," the C.O. called me first as soon as she handed the last piece of non-legal mail out. I knew the drill so without her asking me I signed my name, DOC number and who I received the legal mail from the 19th Judicial Court House.

Before I headed back to my cell block, I stopped to use the phone. I called my family on there instead of using the burner phone. That is one less thing I needed stressing a bitch out. The shit would definitely get back to One. It rang a few times before the operator spoke into my ear.

"You have a collect call from, Cache. If you wish to accept this call, please press one." Before she could say anything else, somebody had accepted the call.

"Girl!" I knew it was my sister, Chanel. She's the only one I know that would answer the phone all ghetto and shit.

"What the fuck you got going on in there? Just like y'all hear shit in there about out here, we hear the same. Then on top of that, why it be taking yo' ass foreva to pick up the phone and dial a bitch up? What you anti-social or something?" She finally caught her breath, giving me a chance to say something.

"Damn, bitch you know I could never be that way with you, but I did not put this money on here for you to be blasting on me. Can you act like you ain't seen or talked to me in forever and show me some love?" I said, laughing.

"You right, I love yo' ass and you know that shit, Cache. Ever since momma died you acting all crazy and shit. And don't think I have not noticed you trying to avoid what I first asked." Her bringing Ann up, really put me in my feelings, with all the shit I had brought upon myself I didn't have the chance to say goodbye.

Sometimes I wonder, though, even if I did have the chance would I have been really ready to let go? Nah, I doubt that me and Ann still had too much to sit, laugh and drink about. I guess God just had other plans for both of us.

"Sis, you tripping. I'm not trying to avoid anything. You know I can handle my own, I just got caught slipping," I responded to what she wanted to clearly know.

"Well, just know I'm willing to catch a charge behind you."

I could tell her not being here for me when shit popped off made her sad. One thing about our family, when one fights, we all dive, so I understood.

"Chill with that, one thing you should know about ya big sis—" I cut myself off realizing I'm on a recorded phone. I changed the subject, "But look, as for me calling, I do what I can. When I get off the phone, my ass gets depressed."

"I thought people in jail usually be blowing up the phones tryna get out that bitch." She caught my drift and no longer questioned me about the fight, good.

"Yeah, they do, sis, but you know I be tryna handle my shit on my own."

"Girl, I respect that, out of all momma kids you have always been the more independent one. It is good to hear from you, though, stranger."

"Yeah, it is from you, too. How is A'nett?" I wanted to cut straight to the chase, the real reason I had made the call.

"She still with Maya. Did you get the letter she wrote?"

"Yeah, I did. I just got it actually, but I haven't had the time to read it yet. What about One? Did she bring A'nett to drop the letter off?" Wondering if she had been letting her go by my people.

"No, girl, A'nett and her went to Mexico on a lil' vacay. I thought you knew that. Maya really has been good to her. She bought her all kinda shit once MoMo C.W. gave her full guardianship."

Right then and there I knew this bitch was still trying to get under my skin and I must admit, she did. I knew the kind of games that she played. She would try and use my daughter to get to me.

"Guardianship? Who the fuck gave them the right to do that shit?" I instantly spazzed out.

I knew that the bitch had my daughter, but legally is a whole different story. She could have never signed shit by right. A'nett was still considered my daughter, I had never given uprights.

"MoMo C.W. shit, you know that woman stuck—"

I cut her off. "I do not give a fuck about her being stuck in shit. Get my fucking daughter now!" I screamed at my sister.

"*Yo' daughter*? Our sister, you mean?" she said, confused.

"Just get her the fuck back. I don't care what you have to do." I slammed the phone so hard, right before I stormed off towards my cell. That quick, the convo with my sister had gone sour.

By the time I made it to my room, I was fuming, burning up with anger.

"Who the fuck are you?" I asked whoever had the balls to be sitting in my cell. I thought I would have to fight once again. This time I would be prepared. When she turned around, I was taken aback by her looks. She looked just like a nigga. *Damn*, was all I could think, but her looks was not what really caught my attention. I knew she had been the one who sent me the breakfast with the note.

"I'm the nigga you been looking for," she said when turning around to face me.

If it was not for this being a women's facility, I would have thought I was in front of a straight up and down man. Her dreads were thick and long, hanging past her shoulders. She had a mouth full of diamonds and she was even physically built like a dude. She still had a soft face, but I could clearly see the hardness in her face. The coldness in her eyes, I would definitely have to see more to convince me *he* had not snuck in my cell to fuck me silly.

"Well, tell me what's up?" I asked tryna see where her head was at.

"You tell me, I know you tryna see what is good with them people," she said, speaking on the hit One sent.

“Why do you give a fuck?” What is your motive?” I knew how these hoes got down in here. I was hip to the bullshit. Always tryna munch off the next bitch and rumor has it I am that bitch. One had to have paid them chickens a pretty penny for them to fuck with me. So, of course, that is why I am checking out this hoe’s angle.

“Let’s just say we have a mutual frenemy we are not really seeing eye to eye with.” She smirked.

“And who may that be?” I questioned her still not trusting anything coming out of her mouth.

“Shit, what you mean who? The one and only One, Maya Hidalgo.”

CHAPTER 40

ONE

Today I planned to chill and relax around the compound. There is nothing like sipping Moscato in your lingerie on the balcony of a mini-mansion looking out at the Caribbean while letting the wind blow your worries away. Only if it was that easy. All my shit back in Louisiana is placed in the backseat while my worries here as of now was staring me in the eye. Emilio and I still hadn't settled our shit. Maybe because I hadn't approached any of it yet. Even though my grandfather knew I was here, we still hadn't laid eyes on one another.

The thing is, I did not have a clue what I would do once I saw him. If I choked the rest of the life that existed out of him within seconds my body would be filled with bullet holes without a thought. That is one reason I had put our time to reunite to the side. I also knew if I waited any longer there was a possibility that I may never get the chance to face this head-on. I knew he had been all my answers to everything I had ever been through. In order to do some healing and soul searching I needed to start with the man right down the hall.

Today just would not be the day. I decided to slip on some clothes instead. I wanted out of my thoughts and the best way to do that was to go and check on A'nett. She had grown accustomed to being here and decided to put her phone down. She started training with some of the trainers around here. I guess she was growing up faster than I thought and expected. For some reason, she was intrigued with guns just as I am, so I knew exactly where to find her.

Once I made it to the gun range in the golf cart, I placed the ear covers over my ears and safety glasses over my eyes. Before I walked upon her, I decided to watch in the shadows to see what she was working with. I waited for the gunshots to pierce my ears. I did not have to wait long either. She had a good stance, arms held how they should be. I watched her inhale and once she exhaled, she pulled the trigger.

The gunshot made my eye twitch, but my heart stayed at a steady pace. The smell of gun powder assaulted my nostrils but in a good way, I craved this sensation. Once her bullet hit its target, I looked to see where it landed. Close, but not quite enough. She did hit the target, but it was not a bull's eye. She knew this is what I expected from her.

"Try to relax and once you do, think of someone that hurt you. Maybe one of them lil' boys back at home." I said walking up on her pushing her hands up a notch. Instead of her responding she did exactly what I said and again she breathed in and out. Then she fired, this time she hit the center of the figure. I smiled. "Damn, A'nett who the hell was you thinking of? I would really hate to be them," I said, laughing but really I wanted to know.

"A boy back at school like you said."

I caught on to her hesitation. I did not push to ask her, though. I just decided to take her word.

"My turn," I said without smiling this time I stepped in her place.

I didn't need to imagine a face because I knew exactly who I wanted dead. Everybody who has ever caused me pain and the list went as far back as my grandfather. I already killed Zane and his boy. The shit they had done to me damaged me for the rest of my life and I could not forgive or forget them. God forgives, not me. I emptied the clip without second thought and I even continued to pull the trigger hoping something would come out.

"Are you alright, Maya?"

"Get yo' fucking hands off me, bitch!" A'nett just stood there speechless, looking at me like I had lost my mind and I did. "I'm sorry, I didn't mean that shit, I just zoned out." I pleaded hoping I didn't need to explain any more than I already have.

She just looked at me without saying anything, I guess she was shocked that I carried it like that. Fuck I was just as surprised. Instead of forgiving me for my outburst, she just stormed off, leaving me standing there with a smoking gun.

***

As I showered, I made up my mind that today would be the day that I went to see my grandfather. I no longer wanted to put it off, it was time. After getting out of the shower I put on something comfortable, but also pretty. I don't know why, but for some strange reason, I felt the need to impress him. I just felt the urge to do so. Before I turned on his side of the compound, I took a deep breath.

"Keep ya' emotions in check, mami," I said aloud, coaching myself.

When I finally made it, two men were guarding the door. They really treated him as if he was the President of the United States or something. I don't think I could ever get used to this. People just did not really live like this, on some make-believe in their own mind, maybe. In the hood the only protection you can truly rely on is your own trigga finger, fuck a bodyguard. If a nigga wanted to hit you where it hurts, it's gonna happen.

"Whoa, whoa. Where are you going?" one of the men asked me, placing his hand to my chest.

"If you don't get ya fucking filthy hands off me. On my life, I will kill you," I said, pushing his hand off me, feeling violated.

"What the hell is going on, out here?" Someone came to the door just in time. My next move was behind my back if his ass decided to jump stupid.

"He put his fucking hands on me," I said, realizing how I sounded like a big ass kid.

"Is that true?" whoever this chick was, asked dude.

"I was just trying to tell her—" He pointed at me. "That she needed to be cleared through us before she could gain access."

"Javier, this is Emilio's granddaughter. Have you lost your mind?"

"Oh, I'm so sorry, ma'am. Please excuse me for my rudeness?" He held out his hand.

I just looked at this fool like he was crazy. I don't know who the fuck he thought I was, but I didn't get notches under my belt for being Emilio's grandchild. I am my own person.

"Come, come." The chick escorted me into Emilio's room, feeling as if she didn't something would pop off. "Please excuse him.

We just employed Javier and besides, he is family. Your cousin to be exact."

I heard what she was saying, but I was not listening. I was too busy looking for my grandfather. Even in his sickness he still looked strong and his presence demanded respect.

"It is not as bad as it may seem, ya know. He is actually doing better. We have been praying for a full recovery and we've employed the best doctors. By the way, my name is Margaret, but everyone calls me Margie." She held her hand out toward me, that is when I noticed how much she looked like me except she was all Spanish like my mom, no Black. Could she be my cousin also?

"I'm your Aunt, your mom's sister," she said answering the question on my mind.

"One, I mean Maya. Nice to meet you. I know exactly who you are. I have been waiting for you ever since you were taken away from us. I'm pretty sure you had no clue I even existed." She smiled politely.

"Nah, actually I haven't." What I really wanted to say was I also didn't trust her. Looking in her eyes I could tell she wasn't the person that beautiful smile or face claimed to be.

CHAPTER 41

CACHE

I am going to assume that Tony is not mad at a bitch, but after our conversation, I'm not sure. He hasn't gotten back with me. Even though he has not picked up the phone to see how a hoe is doing. I wasn't tripping though he was still dropping stacks on my books like it's hot. I know the nigga like the back of my hand. Right now, I bet he was evaluating the situation. Maybe to see if I was worth the drama to put up a fight over. I mean I am his baby momma, that has to count for something. Who can deny a bitch like me, no one! Everything I touch gets stuck like Gucci Mane says, *"You ain't gotta fuck with me, my nigga but you stuck with me."*

Cache rules everything around me. *I gotta make sure I tweet that shit,* I thought smiling to myself. Anyway, back to Tony, I wasn't about to chase behind him at least not at the moment. I had things going on in my life that demanded my full attention as of now. Like getting back at these hoes who put a bitch in the infirmary. In order for me to make that happen, I needed to go see a man about a horse. Ro and I the chick with the teardrops had been planning and plotting an attack on the three bitches responsible. I was ready like a hoe was ready to pop it for a pimp. For the most part, everyone in here respected me, but these three bitches, pulling this shit off made my gutta notches be bumped down a little.

In order for these hoes not to play with me and show respect, I had to get back at them, it was a must. I have always considered myself a fair person, but when bitches pulled my card, I had no problem striking back.

Psst! Psst!

I turned to face who was at my cell door looking for my attention. It could only be one person at this time of the night. Sergeant Johnson, coming to get me to fuck and clean.

"You ready?" he asked me.

Already knowing the answer, he unlocked the door using his key. He usually would tell the control center to pop the cell, but it wasn't that type of night. When you being sneaky, you don't do what is usually done. Without responding I tiptoed off the ladder and out of the room making sure not to wake up my cellmate. I am pretty sure he had all the cameras turned off so that he could cover all of his tracks. What the nigga didn't know is I always covered mines, too. You can never be too sure.

I know Ro had shit in place for when it was time for us to make our move. She was the night orderly, so I knew she had no problem getting around alone with other people. If any of this shit came back on an inmate it would be hard to prove the case, everything would fall back on the free people. Which is one reason we decided to do this shit when the video footage was turned off.

We finally made it to the shakedown room without being detected. The only people up in this bitch was the other muthafuckas who were also trying to get their freak on. See me, I had motive to why I do what I did, most of these hoes fell in love or only be subjected to getting their asses wet. Not a bitch like me. When I stepped inside the room, I could tell Ro had been through to clean. That meant we would not be interrupted by the other orderlies, good.

"I missed you," Johnson said, as soon as we stepped into the room and the door was closed.

He wasn't shy when it came to touching my body and wasted no time for the opportunity. I let him do him with no complaints though, this wasn't something new to me, so I didn't feel uncomfortable. He wasn't attractive in the face, but he had a body like God and a dick like a horse. I certainly wasn't afraid to ride it like a jockey either. Like they say you never know all the things you will miss when you are locked up and dick was one thing I needed. Whenever we linked up, I always savored the moment. I am definitely determined to keep a dick in here for the next fifteen years if I have to. I also had a backup plan like Soulja Slim for everyone I lose I bounce back with two.

As he kissed my neck, one hand continued to get to know the curves of my shapely body, while the other played hide and seek in my juicy tunnel.

"Damn, Cache, you wet, wet. You must have missed me too, baby?"

"Fucking right! Do yo' shit, Johnson. Make this pussy come," I moaned not really listening to what he said.

He played with my pussy until I came hard on his fingers. By this time his dick was rock hard standing at attention. I was also just as ready as he appeared to be. You would think that we would be trying to catch our nut and get the fuck out, but his ass acted like he wanted to make love to my pussy. We didn't get to do this too often either, so I was down for foreplay.

"Take off your clothes and grab your ankles," he demanded.

It was something about a man being aggressive toward my pussy that turned me on. Without objection from my end, I did what I was told, making sure I was as naked as the day I was born. I grabbed my ankles on the way down making sure to spread my legs apart. Once I was in position, he came from around his back with two shiny cuffs. First standing on my right side he cuffed my wrists then connected the other cuff to my ankle. Then he walked to my left and did the same. I usually played the dominator part but for whatever reason, I went along with what he wanted. Even though I had never played cops and robbers with him I was excited to see what I was getting myself into. Maybe what really turned me on was the payback I'd be dishing out tonight. That shit really excited me.

Once I had been detained, I could see his movements through the darkness while peeking through my legs. The light that also shined through the small window from the hallway helped. I waited to see what would happen next. He pulled up a chair behind me, maybe the same one we used a time before maybe not. All I knew was last time he fucked me so good on it, my pussy instantly started pulsating when I saw it.

I didn't have to wonder for long. "Don't run."

"I won't," was all I got to say before he spread my ass cheeks as far as they would go diving headfirst like he was competing in the Olympic game. I couldn't do anything but take that shit even if I wanted to run, it wasn't happening.

"Yes," I moaned almost not able to keep my voice down. If you asked me, Johnson didn't care at least that what it seemed like. Just as his dick was rock hard, so was his tongue. His tongue slithered like a snake gliding in and out each of my holes. It didn't take long for me to feel myself about to cum, this nigga was driving me wild. I was even seeing stars I had cum so much in less than ten minutes.

"Don't you fucking move!" I screamed this time I was squirting all over his face.

I fell to the floor not able to stand anymore. My knees were weak but that didn't stop me. As soon as the cuffs came off, I attacked him like a caged animal. I soon found out why he decided to cuff me. I did exactly what he expected me to do. I rode the dick like it was the last one on Earth.

***

After Johnson and I finished fucking, he left me in the shakedown room to get dressed. Before I left out of the room, I grabbed my phone from where Ro said it would be recording us. This was my leverage for the shit to not fall back on me. He would definitely be playing a part, if not he would not only lose his job and have to register as a sex offender for the rest of his life, but I doubt he wanted back up time for fucking with a bitch like me.

"Ayo," Ro said stepping through the door letting me know she was there.

"You can turn around I'm dressed."

"You good, everything straight?" she asked me.

"Yeah, I did what I had to. What about you, we good?" I asked wondering if she handled her part.

"No doubt. Let's go back to our block because in a couple of hours she gon' pop off."

"Aight, let me take a quick shower because I know soon the cameras will be back on." I didn't know what she meant by shit popping off and I don't think it was something we needed to talk about either. We went our separate ways without saying nothing else.

CHAPTER 42

TONY

I received a call from my lawyer earlier this morning telling me that all state charges had been dropped against me and I was a free man. He must have been reading my mind because I had definitely planned to go see him today. That was a sure sign that it was time for me to go handle my business. I drove up to the airport making a quick dash into the terminal before I missed my flight. I was headed out to Tijuana, Mexico to meet the boss. He was a major player in the game and supplied a selected few throughout the US. I felt privileged to be fucking with the plug. There wasn't many hustlers alive that could testify to meeting the man.

For the ones that has had the chance to come in contact with him said he is a rambunctious man. He didn't fuck with many especially on a personal level, but he always put his business first. He was 'bout his money and so was I, the feeling was mutual. I had to get it how I lived, no questions asked. I boarded the plane, turned off my phone, found my seat closest to the window and plugged in my iPod.

***

After hours of riding in the air, the plane had finally landed on the soil of Tijuana. The sight was breathtaking. The smell of the salt in the ocean water was relaxing. I could even smell the money, that would soon be rolling in and thought about the fact that my nigga couldn't be here with me. I'ma still make sure I live out what we were both aiming to accomplish. I knew my nigga was watching over me. I still had niggas on top of that shit for me to find his killer. That's just something I could never let slide.

I made my way to the car garage like I was told. I looked around to see where my ride was. I wasn't given an address to go to but was told to wait. I didn't have to wait for long. As soon as I stepped through the exit, an all-black Mercedes Benz pulled up in front of me. I didn't move, I wasn't sure if the ride was mine or not.

"Get in. What you waiting on, Papi?"

That was my cue. As soon as my ass hit the seat and my door was shut, we pulled away from the airport as quick as they had come. I looked over to see a bitch with a banging body and a face to match. No words were exchanged, and I also felt none was needed. I did check her fine ass out, though. She had on French designer Christian Dior with black red bottom heels. The bitch was a work of art and I could tell she had class. This was far from what I was used to, and I have had some bad hoes. I wondered what dick she had to suck or was she blood-related. Whoever she was did not matter because I didn't plan to mix business with pleasure.

As we cruised down the streets of Tijuana, my mind drifted off to my life back home and where I was headed. By thirty-five, my plans were to be able to lay back and enjoy the fruits of my hustle. I could also see myself married with kids. I hadn't met anyone yet that held my attention long enough for me to feel they were the ones that deserved the Kidd for that matter. No one except Cache, I knew her like I know myself. Or at least that is what I thought. All the shit she laid on me the other night, really fucked my head up. I wasn't sure if I could trust her as far as I could throw her. As I said I respected her hustle, but right game, wrong nigga.

Not saying I forgot where I came from, fuck I know the struggle. The shit, like she said, I was doing ain't no better. Especially now that I am about to flood the streets like it is the eighties. I guess that's the pot calling the kettle black. A hustle is a hustle is a hustle, so who am I to judge. When we pulled up to the beautifully equipped mansion, I took a look around. I admired the beachfront styled home. I pictured something like this belonging to me one day.

"I'm guessing you like what you see, Papi?" Not giving me time to answer she continued, "Tomorrow you do business, tonight you relax," she said as we stepped outside of the Benz.

As she escorted me to the front entrance, before we could make it to the door we were greeted by an exotic woman with a big smile, big breasts and of course a phat ass. Oh, let me not forget my favorite drink, Ciroc, a man couldn't ask for more. As I accepted my drink, I could not help but check her out. She was even thicker than the honey I rode with. Maybe it was the two-piece swimsuit that hugged every curve just right. She also sported chocolate diamonds which reflected off the color of her creamy skin. The gold Louboutin red bottom pumps didn't make it any easier for me either. She looked damn good, I had to adjust myself.

"Mr. Clark, stop drooling. Have as much fun with her as you would like. Remember she is here to please you and there is no such thing as not mixing business with pleasure. It is our pleasure to do business."

After that, we were both left alone, and I definitely wasn't no punk when it came to pussy. Tonight, I would not think about Cache, but instead, enjoy the pleasure of doing business.

***

The next morning, I got up, it was time to handle business. After taking a shower I put on a YSL white tee with some YSL jeans and every hustler's trademark kicks, Air Force Ones, all-white. I topped it off with some Issy Miyake cologne and was ready for the day. When I entered the island-style kitchen, I was greeted with the smell of bacon, eggs, bagel, and fresh fruit. I had always seen on TV how rich muthafuckas fixed all kinda foods to feed a nation, only for it all to go to waste, but I guess this is the life of a king. I didn't have the stomach for food, so instead, I decided to make my way outback. I wanted to view the ocean water I was told it was a peaceful time to do so.

I found my mind drifting once again back to Cache. This time I pictured her walking, toes in the sand with a laced, all-white Alexander McQueen dress, hair flowing and all. I could even see her carrying my baby. I smiled because I knew that is exactly what she deserved.

"I'm glad you finally decided to join me. I have been sitting here watching your mind drift with the ocean."

I turned to see a different woman than the first two that I had already encountered.

"I'm Margaret and I'm here on the behalf of my father to speak business. Emilio Hidalgo sends his respect."

I nodded to acknowledge the words that she spoke. Her face was familiar, but I could not recall where I'd seen her. All I knew was something about her made me feel uneasy. Maybe it was the scar across her face. Even though she was still beautiful I could see beyond her smile.

She held her hand out for me to shake. I took it into my own without thinking twice, regardless of how I felt at the end of the day this was business. As I said it always comes before pleasure.

CHAPTER 43

CACHE

The next morning when I woke up, well when the morning rolls around because I definitely did not sleep. I was anticipating what would *pop off.* Ro did not tell me what would come, so I was alert. I looked at the clock on the wall outside of my cell and saw that it was 6:15. It was shift change and count time. I had no idea what Ro could have done, maybe tied them hoes up and beat their asses. Who knows? One thing for sure soon enough I would find out. I'd heard around the jail how vicious she could be, so this would tell if the rumors were true or not. Whatever she had planned the only thing I could do was trust that her ass would handle business.

I could not sleep but I decided to just lay there looking at the walls and all the writing. I refused to place my thoughts or name upon them. Not that I believed in if I leave my name I will come back to jail. It is just these walls told a story of its own and my story would not be left because this is not what I want to be remembered by.

"Aaahhh! Oh my God, somebody help!"

I jumped out of my bed looking around, becoming alert. My heart jumped damn near out my chest. I knew that was my cue that the shit was going down. I ran to my cell door because I wanted to see what was going on. My cell was locked. So, this was as far as I could go.

"Lockdown! Everyone on your fucking bunks, get the fuck on your bunks now!"

There was commotion everywhere, but I still could not see any movement.

"Bunkie, what the fuck's going on?" she asked rubbing sleep from her eyes.

"I don't know, but they said to stay on the bunks," I said, not wanting this hoe to crowd my space.

"Sounds to me that it might be a shakedown," she said getting up to pee. "Girl let me use this bathroom, fix me a cup of coffee and grab my radio before they have a bitch sitting out on the hall all fucking day."

I continued to look on to see if they were headed our way. One thing for sure if this was a shake down, I had all my shit hid behind the light fixture. That was the least of my worries. Before I could register what was happening, I saw a cloud of smoke and that's when my lungs started getting tight. Like someone was sitting on my chest making my chest cave in. They must have thrown a smoke bomb. I grabbed my chest trying not to breathe in as much, but the more I tried the more I did. My Bunkie fell from the toilet. Someone was at my cell door because I could hear keys. My vision had become so blurry I could not see who was coming. I felt someone's hands grab me placing me in cuffs, but before they could lock my other hand, without warning I had hit the floor.

***

"Welcome back."

I looked up looking in the eyes of a tall, dark, man in a suit with cheap shoes and cologne that reminded me of Raid.

"I hope you know you are in a shitload of shit and if I was you, I would start talking."

I just looked at this nigga if I was to guess he was a cop, but why would he be here?

"You don't want to talk?'

"Who are you? And what would you like me to talk about? All the fuck I know is I don't know shit."

"Oh, so you one of those types, huh? Sticking to the gee code. The code of silence, huh? By the way to answer your question I am Detective Adams, Detective John Adams," he said, pulling out his badge.

I knew I was right, I know a cop from anywhere.

"I knew I smelled stale coffee and doughnuts." I laughed just for the hell of it, not that I found anything humorous. Whatever it is that Ro had done I had no clue what it was so even if I wanted to talk, I did not know shit.

"Alright suit yourself, call your lawyer Robert whenever you want to cop a deal," he said, standing up to make his exit.

"A deal for what? Not that I'm interested." I looked at him smirking before he could leave.

Without missing a beat, he smiled back. "Oh, it's no big deal, ya know," he said, with his last two words trying to sound hood. "Just a double homicide."

Before I could even fix my mouth to say anything the detective left me with my mouth wide open. The thing is, I was not talking and did not plan to. Shit had definitely popped off like fireworks, but it was not the Fourth of July.

CHAPTER 44

RO

The next morning came faster than expected. You know when you are usually waiting on something the time drags. I smiled wickedly because I could not wait until the time came. One thing I knew Cache would definitely be inspired by my actions. I decided that killing all three girls would not only be foolish, but it was not worth it either. But I knew in order to gain some order I had to knock the head off and the body would fall. That's exactly what I had done.

The three chicks that were involved were Diamond, Jaika, and Ke'aira. There is one thing that will always remain about prison, a secret is never a secret including what I had done, truth be told as long as I stayed solid and true to myself I knew I was good. No camera, no witnesses, no case.

Jaikia was the ringleader of the crew, so I knew from the jump she was the one that had to go. For weeks I seduced the broad by playing on her emotional state. I knew how she felt about me and that only made it easier to get in where I fit in. I hit her off with what she wanted, some good ole country dick. I was known for making *straps*, a detachable penis, in the pen and fucking these hoes silly.Next thing I knew she was all in love with the kid, doing any and everything I wanted. The bitch kinda reminded me of the chick off *Coming to America.* If I asked her to hop on one leg and start barking like a dog then my wish would be her command.

What I did was easy I just waited closer to the time I knew Sergeant Johnson and Cache would be finished fucking. Word around the prison was that Johnson's freaky ass had been fucking a few bitches around here. I knew about him and Jaikia because one night about a week ago when we were pillow talking, she spilled the beans. That is what Xanax did to you, though. I fixed her a nice cup of coffee and crushed the pills mixing them into her drink. The pills made her relax. She told me everything by first starting with how she could not wait until we got home. Thinking I would be with her. Then out of the blue tears started streaming down her face and she told me she had a confession. I was not really listening because I knew that is how Xanax had you, all emotional and shit. That was until she brought Johnson's name in the picture.

She started confessing to me about how she had been fucking him, even right after me and that she was, in fact, carrying his child. She said the only reason she did the job on Cache that Maya sent was because she would need the money. Johnson would not take care of them and she refused to abort. What she didn't know was I would do what I had to do to get in Cache's good grace. I was ready to go to war with God behind her. Maya was the reason. When we were together, she would go on and on about the infamous Cache that one night I felt I wanted to have my cake and eat it, too.

I didn't know that one day we would end up locked up together, so when the opportunity came, I jumped on it. When all this shit happened with Cache I took that as the perfect opportunity to go with my move. I did think sending the breakfast was just a lil' too much, but I also wanted her to see I was also running things inside these walls just as she was.

I continued to sit in my cell, naked with my dreads pulled into a messy bun. I knew soon that someone would soon be coming for me. I wasn't too much worried about the shit, though, because the only people that knew what I had done was me, Cache, Jaikia and Sergeant Johnson. I didn't expect the dead to talk. When I looked up from the People's magazine, it was because the shouting got louder. There standing in front of my cell was Warden Lane, correctional officers, and two uniform cops. I placed the People's magazine down on the bunk, stood up, got on my knees, and placed my hands on my head. I already knew what time it was. The officer opened my cell as the other rushed in.

Once they saw I did not pose a threat. I was pushed down to the floor, headfirst. They wanted a reaction out of me, but I refused to give them what they wanted. I would remain silent because I would not be proven guilty. I would not say a word. As I said, no camera, no witnesses, no case. As for Cache, I knew she is a rider and had the code of silence embedded in her DNA.

CHAPTER 45

MAYA

Back at The Compound

For some reason, I could not trust my loving aunt Margaret. If she was anything like me or Emilio, then that answered my question? She was a force to be reckoned with. I knew the apple didn't fall far from tree. What I did not understand was, if she knew so much about me, why she never made herself known? Why she never came for me and I knew nothing at all about her? Didn't even know she existed. For crying out loud I am her only sister's daughter. That had to count for something, right? In Mexico, La Familia supposed to mean everything, and blood is always thicker than water. Of course, my grandfather had taken that birthright from me when he killed my parents. Fuck La Familia! As for my aunt, I knew absolutely nothing about Margaret, but I definitely planned to find out what I needed to know, and soon.

Today I decided to do a little self-relaxation and stay in. The first thing I had done was make a house call so that some people could come over and give me a Brazilian wax, a facial and to get my body rubbed with hot scented oils.

Rip! I winced in pain as the wax strip was pulled and the hair had been removed. I had taken it like a gee, though, beauty could be painful.

"Miss Hidalgo, we need you pronto!" One of the house servants came storming inside jarring me. The first thing that popped in my head was my grandfather had finally decided to die.

We all rushed out of the room immediately, but we did not go the way my grandfather was being hospitalized. This had me wondering what could possibly have them this alert if it wasn't, Emilio? We finally made it to the suite that A'nett had been staying in, the door was open but I still couldn't see. Everyone had stopped, daring to go inside. I felt as if I was in slow motion, swiping them all out of my way so that I could pass through.

Kicked over in the middle of the floor was a chair. That is when my eyes traveled up to A'nett's feet, from her legs to her torso. All of a sudden that is when my eyes bypassed everything else and around her neck, a white sheet was tied.

***

Back to Baton Rouge

A Week Later

This is the hardest thing I think I have ever had to do in my life. For one I had been given the authority over someone's life. To protect and care for and I could not even do that, I fucked up, I know I did. For a while, I'd been out for revenge to hurt Cache because that is what I felt was appropriate. Just as I had failed her daughter, on the night I had been raped, she failed me. In my heart, I knew I could not compare the two, but she just don't know how that night affected me. But this was not about neither me nor Cache. A'nett trusted me not only as her guardian but as a mother figure. The shit is really hard for me to think about. I know I let her down and Momo C.W. was even counting on me. Even though she did not comprehend what had unfolded around her, I still felt fucked up.

A week has passed since this unexpected tragedy has happened with A'nett. Today she will be laid to rest and that means Cache and I will meet face to face. The prison will allow her to attend by A'nett legally being her daughter. I did think about not showing my face, but I had every right to be there. I also did not want to look guilty as if I did something wrong, knowing I did not. If for no other reason I owe A'nett that respect at least.

A'nett left a suicide letter, which after reading I mailed it to Cache. Fuck, what else was I to do? I didn't know how else I would tell her, and she deserved to know. I know we have been through shit in the past, but as I said her child has nothing to do with our unsettled beef. After getting dressed I was prepared to leave and head to the homecoming. When I opened the door, I noticed how grayish and gloomy-looking the sky had become. The scenery is only an alliance to the emotions of so many who held A'nett dear to their heart, including me. I continued my way despite how I felt, but not before checking my gun. This is a day of pain and one thing I know from experience is hurt people hurt people.

I know attending the funeral could mean a dismissal for me, but I am prepared to take the chance even if it means losing my life in the process. I knew for a fact that Tony and I would cross each other today. I just hoped he had the decency and respect not to pop off at a time like this. To be honest I hope that I can behave myself because my trigger finger is telling a different story. I would hate to turn this farewell into a battlefield. If things do get ugly I'd be prepared for whatever, though. It will be me or him and I'd never been the type of bitch to lay flat.

Besides, it's time I showed this nigga who he was really fucking with. If it wasn't for him, we wouldn't be here. I can't just blame him, though, because Cache's promiscuous ways is really what got the ball rolling. But all is fair in love and war. Once I pulled up to the church, I knew there was no turning back. This would either be a fresh start to new beginnings or the end of everything. Only time will tell, I just prayed someone from a higher power forgives me of my trespasses because for me it's hard to forgive those who has trespassed against me.

To Be Continued...
C.R.E.A.M. 2
Coming Soon

Submission Guideline

Submit the first three chapters of your completed manuscript to ldpsubmissions@gmail.com, subject line: Your book's title. The manuscript must be in a .doc file and sent as an attachment. Document should be in Times New Roman, double spaced and in size 12 font. Also, provide your synopsis and full contact information. If sending multiple submissions, they must each be in a separate email.

Have a story but no way to send it electronically? You can still submit to LDP/Ca$h Presents. Send in the first three chapters, written or typed, of your completed manuscript to:

LDP: Submissions Dept
Po Box 944
Stockbridge, Ga 30281

DO NOT send original manuscript. Must be a duplicate.

Provide your synopsis and a cover letter containing your full contact information.

Thanks for considering LDP and Ca$h Presents.

Coming Soon from Lock Down Publications/Ca$h Presents

BOW DOWN TO MY GANGSTA

By **Ca$h**

TORN BETWEEN TWO

By **Coffee**

THE STREETS STAINED MY SOUL **II**

By **Marcellus Allen**

BLOOD OF A BOSS **VI**

SHADOWS OF THE GAME II

By **Askari**

LOYAL TO THE GAME **IV**

By **T.J. & Jelissa**

A DOPEBOY'S PRAYER **II**

By **Eddie "Wolf" Lee**

IF LOVING YOU IS WRONG… **III**

By **Jelissa**

TRUE SAVAGE **VII**

MIDNIGHT CARTEL III

DOPE BOY MAGIC IV

CITY OF KINGZ II

By **Chris Green**

BLAST FOR ME **III**

A SAVAGE DOPEBOY III

CUTTHROAT MAFIA III

By **Ghost**

A HUSTLER'S DECEIT III

KILL ZONE **II**

BAE BELONGS TO ME III

A DOPE BOY'S QUEEN III

By **Aryanna**

COKE KINGS V

KING OF THE TRAP II

By **T.J. Edwards**

GORILLAZ IN THE BAY V

De'Kari

THE STREETS ARE CALLING II

Duquie Wilson

KINGPIN KILLAZ IV

STREET KINGS III

PAID IN BLOOD III

CARTEL KILLAZ IV

DOPE GODS III

Hood Rich

SINS OF A HUSTLA II

ASAD

KINGZ OF THE GAME V

Playa Ray

SLAUGHTER GANG IV

RUTHLESS HEART IV

By Willie Slaughter

THE HEART OF A SAVAGE III

By Jibril Williams

FUK SHYT II

By Blakk Diamond

THE REALEST KILLAZ III

By Tranay Adams

TRAP GOD III

By Troublesome

YAYO IV

C.R.E.A.M.

A SHOOTER'S AMBITION III

By S. Allen

GHOST MOB

Stilloan Robinson

KINGPIN DREAMS III

By Paper Boi Rari

CREAM II

By Yolanda Moore

SON OF A DOPE FIEND III

By Renta

FOREVER GANGSTA II

GLOCKS ON SATIN SHEETS III

By Adrian Dulan

LOYALTY AIN'T PROMISED II

By Keith Williams

THE PRICE YOU PAY FOR LOVE II

By Destiny Skai

CONFESSIONS OF A GANGSTA II

By Nicholas Lock

I'M NOTHING WITHOUT HIS LOVE II

By Monet Dragun

LIFE OF A SAVAGE IV

A GANGSTA'S QUR'AN II

MURDA SEASON II

GANGLAND CARTEL II

By **Romell Tukes**

QUIET MONEY III

THUG LIFE II

By **Trai'Quan**

THE STREETS MADE ME III

By **Larry D. Wright**

THE ULTIMATE SACRIFICE VI

IF YOU CROSS ME ONCE II

ANGEL III

By **Anthony Fields**

THE LIFE OF A HOOD STAR

By Ca$h & Rashia Wilson

FRIEND OR FOE II

By **Mimi**

SAVAGE STORMS II

By **Meesha**

BLOOD ON THE MONEY II

By J-Blunt

THE STREETS WILL NEVER CLOSE II

By K'ajji

Available Now

RESTRAINING ORDER **I & II**

By **CA$H & Coffee**

LOVE KNOWS NO BOUNDARIES **I II & III**

By **Coffee**

RAISED AS A GOON I, II, III & IV

BRED BY THE SLUMS I, II, III

BLAST FOR ME I & II

ROTTEN TO THE CORE I II III

A BRONX TALE I, II, III

DUFFEL BAG CARTEL I II III IV

HEARTLESS GOON I II III IV

A SAVAGE DOPEBOY I II

HEARTLESS GOON I II III

DRUG LORDS I II III

CUTTHROAT MAFIA I II

By **Ghost**

LAY IT DOWN **I & II**

LAST OF A DYING BREED

BLOOD STAINS OF A SHOTTA I & II III

By **Jamaica**

LOYAL TO THE GAME I II III

LIFE OF SIN I, II III

By **TJ & Jelissa**

BLOODY COMMAS I & II

SKI MASK CARTEL I II & III

KING OF NEW YORK I II,III IV V

RISE TO POWER I II III

COKE KINGS I II III IV

BORN HEARTLESS I II III IV

KING OF THE TRAP

By **T.J. Edwards**

IF LOVING HIM IS WRONG…I & II

LOVE ME EVEN WHEN IT HURTS I II III

By **Jelissa**

WHEN THE STREETS CLAP BACK I & II III

THE HEART OF A SAVAGE I II

By **Jibril Williams**

A DISTINGUISHED THUG STOLE MY HEART I II & III

LOVE SHOULDN'T HURT I II III IV
RENEGADE BOYS I II III IV
PAID IN KARMA I II III
SAVAGE STORMS
By **Meesha**
A GANGSTER'S CODE I &, II III
A GANGSTER'S SYN I II III
THE SAVAGE LIFE I II III
CHAINED TO THE STREETS I II III
BLOOD ON THE MONEY
By J-Blunt
PUSH IT TO THE LIMIT
By **Bre' Hayes**
BLOOD OF A BOSS **I, II, III, IV, V**
SHADOWS OF THE GAME
By **Askari**
THE STREETS BLEED MURDER **I, II & III**
THE HEART OF A GANGSTA I II& III
By **Jerry Jackson**
CUM FOR ME I II III IV V
An **LDP Erotica Collaboration**
BRIDE OF A HUSTLA **I II & II**
THE FETTI GIRLS **I, II& III**
CORRUPTED BY A GANGSTA I, II III, IV
BLINDED BY HIS LOVE
THE PRICE YOU PAY FOR LOVE
DOPE GIRL MAGIC I II III
By **Destiny Skai**
WHEN A GOOD GIRL GOES BAD
By **Adrienne**

C.R.E.A.M.

THE COST OF LOYALTY I II III

By Kweli

A GANGSTER'S REVENGE **I II III & IV**

THE BOSS MAN'S DAUGHTERS I II III IV V

A SAVAGE LOVE **I & II**

BAE BELONGS TO ME I II

A HUSTLER'S DECEIT I, II, III

WHAT BAD BITCHES DO I, II, III

SOUL OF A MONSTER I II III

KILL ZONE

A DOPE BOY'S QUEEN I II

By **Aryanna**

A KINGPIN'S AMBITON

A KINGPIN'S AMBITION **II**

I MURDER FOR THE DOUGH

By **Ambitious**

TRUE SAVAGE I II III IV V VI

DOPE BOY MAGIC I, II, III

MIDNIGHT CARTEL I II

CITY OF KINGZ

By **Chris Green**

A DOPEBOY'S PRAYER

By **Eddie "Wolf" Lee**

THE KING CARTEL **I, II & III**

By **Frank Gresham**

THESE NIGGAS AIN'T LOYAL **I, II & III**

By **Nikki Tee**

GANGSTA SHYT **I II &III**

By **CATO**

THE ULTIMATE BETRAYAL

By **Phoenix**

BOSS'N UP **I , II & III**

By **Royal Nicole**

I LOVE YOU TO DEATH

By Destiny J

I RIDE FOR MY HITTA

I STILL RIDE FOR MY HITTA

By **Misty Holt**

LOVE & CHASIN' PAPER

By **Qay Crockett**

TO DIE IN VAIN

SINS OF A HUSTLA

By **ASAD**

BROOKLYN HUSTLAZ

By **Boogsy Morina**

BROOKLYN ON LOCK I & II

By **Sonovia**

GANGSTA CITY

By **Teddy Duke**

A DRUG KING AND HIS DIAMOND I & II III

A DOPEMAN'S RICHES

HER MAN, MINE'S TOO I, II

CASH MONEY HO'S

By Nicole Goosby

TRAPHOUSE KING **I II & III**

KINGPIN KILLAZ I II III

STREET KINGS I II

PAID IN BLOOD **I II**

CARTEL KILLAZ I II III

DOPE GODS I II

By **Hood Rich**

LIPSTICK KILLAH **I, II, III**

CRIME OF PASSION I II & III

FRIEND OR FOE

By **Mimi**

STEADY MOBBN' **I, II, III**

THE STREETS STAINED MY SOUL

By **Marcellus Allen**

WHO SHOT YA **I, II, III**

SON OF A DOPE FIEND I II

Renta

GORILLAZ IN THE BAY **I II III IV**

TEARS OF A GANGSTA I II

DE'KARI

TRIGGADALE I II III

Elijah R. Freeman

GOD BLESS THE TRAPPERS I, II, III

THESE SCANDALOUS STREETS I, II, III

FEAR MY GANGSTA I, II, III IV, V

THESE STREETS DON'T LOVE NOBODY I, II

BURY ME A G I, II, III, IV, V

A GANGSTA'S EMPIRE I, II, III, IV

THE DOPEMAN'S BODYGAURD I II

THE REALEST KILLAZ I II

Tranay Adams

THE STREETS ARE CALLING

Duquie Wilson

MARRIED TO A BOSS… I II III

By Destiny Skai & Chris Green

KINGZ OF THE GAME I II III IV

Playa Ray

SLAUGHTER GANG I II III

RUTHLESS HEART I II III

By Willie Slaughter

FUK SHYT

By Blakk Diamond

DON'T F#CK WITH MY HEART I II

By Linnea

ADDICTED TO THE DRAMA I II III

By Jamila

YAYO I II III

A SHOOTER'S AMBITION I II

By S. Allen

TRAP GOD I II

By Troublesome

FOREVER GANGSTA

GLOCKS ON SATIN SHEETS I II

By Adrian Dulan

TOE TAGZ I II III

By Ah'Million

KINGPIN DREAMS I II

By Paper Boi Rari

CONFESSIONS OF A GANGSTA

By Nicholas Lock

I'M NOTHING WITHOUT HIS LOVE

By Monet Dragun

CAUGHT UP IN THE LIFE I II III

By Robert Baptiste

NEW TO THE GAME I II III

By **Malik D. Rice**

LIFE OF A SAVAGE I II III

A GANGSTA'S QUR'AN

MURDA SEASON

GANGLAND CARTEL

By **Romell Tukes**

LOYALTY AIN'T PROMISED

By Keith Williams

QUIET MONEY I II

THUG LIFE

By **Trai'Quan**

THE STREETS MADE ME I II

By **Larry D. Wright**

THE ULTIMATE SACRIFICE I, II, III, IV, V

KHADIFI

IF YOU CROSS ME ONCE

ANGEL I II

By **Anthony Fields**

THE LIFE OF A HOOD STAR

By Ca$h & Rashia Wilson

THE STREETS WILL NEVER CLOSE

By K'ajji

CREAM

By Yolanda Moore

BOOKS BY LDP'S CEO, CA$H

TRUST IN NO MAN

TRUST IN NO MAN 2

TRUST IN NO MAN 3

BONDED BY BLOOD

SHORTY GOT A THUG

THUGS CRY

THUGS CRY 2

THUGS CRY 3

TRUST NO BITCH

TRUST NO BITCH 2

TRUST NO BITCH 3

TIL MY CASKET DROPS

RESTRAINING ORDER

RESTRAINING ORDER 2

IN LOVE WITH A CONVICT

LIFE OF A HOOD STAR

Coming Soon

BONDED BY BLOOD 2

BOW DOWN TO MY GANGSTA